TILTAWHIRL JOHN

He didn't plan it. It just seemed that when you're a hair short of sixteen it's time to go out and see a bit of the world. So he ran away, stuck out his thumb, and hitched a ride to the first "Hiring" sign that caught his eye. That was how he ended up working on a beet farm, hoeing endless lines of beets from dawn to dusk, sleeping on a hardwood floor, and living on beans and stale bread. And how he learned how cruel a man could be—and how easy to kill. The beet farm took him to rock bottom. Then Tiltawhirl John picked him up. T-John knew every scam and stunt in the book. Because T-John was a carnie man, running the Tiltawhirl in a traveling carnival, running carnie scams, and then moving on. And it wasn't long before the kid was a carnie, too, and wasn't that the life. But there was one thing the kid didn't know, that T-John had still to teach him. One thing that would tilt the world on its head and change the kid's life forever.

OTHER PUFFIN BOOKS BY GARY PAULSEN

Tiltawhirl John

Gary Paulsen

PUFFIN BOOKS

PUFFIN BOOKS

Published by the Penguin Group

Viking Penguin, a division of Penguin Books USA Inc.,

375 Hudson Street, New York, New York 10014, U.S.A.

Penguin Books Ltd, 27 Wrights Lane, London W8 5TZ, England

Penguin Books Australia Ltd, Ringwood, Victoria, Australia

Penguin Books Canada Ltd, 2801 John Street, Markham, Ontario, Canada L3R 1B4

Penguin Books (N.Z.) Ltd, 182–190 Wairau Road, Auckland 10, New Zealand

Penguin Books Ltd, Registered Offices: Harmondsworth, Middlesex, England

First published in the United States of America by Thomas Nelson Publishers, 1977
Published in Puffin Books 1990
1 3 5 7 9 10 8 6 4 2
Copyright © Gary Paulsen, 1977

No character in this book is intended to represent any actual person;
all the incidents of the story are entirely fictional in nature.

LIBRARY OF CONGRESS CATALOGING IN PUBLICATION DATA

Paulsen, Gary.   Tiltawhirl John / by Gary Paulsen.   p.   cm.

Summary: A fifteen-year-old runaway discovers that a carnival's
razzle-dazzle doesn't shield it from the cruelties of life.

ISBN 0-14-034312-1

[1. Carnivals—Fiction.   2. Runaways—Fiction.]   I. Title.

PZ7.P2843Ti 1990   [Fic]—dc20   90-32602

Printed in the United States of America
Set in Century Schoolbook

This book is dedicated to
Ruth and Gito,
the only two
who have ever meant anything to me;
with deep love.

Tiltawhirl
John

★ 1 ★

It was in the summer when I came onto being sixteen that I ran off and met Tiltawhirl John and learned all about life and sex and what it meant to be a man.

Of course I didn't set out to do it, didn't just suddenly sit down and say, Now that I'm fifteen and close as hair to sixteen I think I'll run off and learn all about sex and life and what it's like not just to be a man, but to kill a man, and to fall in love, and to see so much of the wrong side of people that I'm not sure I want to be a person.

I didn't plan any of it, and if you want to know the iron truth of it all, if I *had* known what was coming I don't think I would have done it. I think I would have just stayed home, bad as it was, and gone to school to make up my grades and grown up and married Elaine Peterson whom I loved then but don't anymore.

Because when you get right down to it there was more sour than there was sweet to the whole affair.

9

And unless your mind is upside down, you don't want to go around sucking a vinegar rag *all* the time—now and then you like a lick of honey. But when I close my eyes, or sometimes when I dream, all I get for memories are the sour tastes, and none of the good things that happened come through.

Maybe that will change when I get old; maybe when I'm twenty-five I'll be able to look back and like what happened, or parts of it. I hope so, because, like I said, if I had it to do over again I'd back off and let it happen without me.

"I've been dumb and I've been smart," T-John, which is what Tiltawhirl John liked to be called, used to say. "And I like smart better."

And it could be that running off when I came onto sixteen made me smarter—I learned some things I didn't know before—but I'm not sure T-John was right. I'm not sure it's good to be smarter, because sometimes it's like getting hit with a hammer because it feels good when you stop. That whole business of getting smarter is like the hammer, and it comes to me now and then that it might be better just to stay dumb and not get hit with the hammer.

But like I said, I didn't plan any of it. It just happened, like rain, and there wasn't anything I could do about it.

There came a day when my Uncle Ernest, who never liked to be called Ernie, took me out in the grass of the lawn next to the house and sat me down and told me that he was giving me eighty acres of flat ground, good ground, and that I could farm it any way I liked, because I was a man and would have to plan on someday taking over the farm and this would be a good way to start.

So I'd lived with Ernest and Florence Peterson, who didn't have any kids of their own, ever since I was little and my folks, whom I didn't remember, had died. They were like my parents, but even so, it was wrong to give me that land.

Wrong because I was too young and hadn't been anywhere but on a wheat farm in northeastern North Dakota. Wrong because I didn't know anything but the farm. Wrong because I wasn't ready and needed more time to figure out even if I wanted to be a farmer or not, because Willy Jackson, who'd left home the year before, came back that year with a neat new car, and he told me stories about girls in Minneapolis where he got a job in a refrigerator factory. Well, that part doesn't matter and makes no never mind. Those girls are the kind that make staying on the farm a little hard when your uncle tries to give you eighty acres of flat ground and tells you to settle down.

Then there's this business of fame and fortune. I know it sounds dumb, but if you just take eighty acres from your uncle, even if he is just like your father, and you settle down on those eighty acres, well, you'll never know if you can do anything on your own. You just know what you can do when it's handed to you on a platter.

So you can see why I had to leave, and I decided to go west because that's where the money was. Well, not really west, just western North Dakota, where there was farm work in the spring and where, I'd heard, they were so hard up for workers they didn't ask too many questions. They had a bumper crop of sugar beets going, and if they didn't get the workers to thin them by hand, the only way, they'd lose the crop.

So one morning in May, when Ernest and Florence were gone for the day to look at some new stock, I left a note and went out on the highway west of town with a boxful of clothes and cans of sardines for food and held out my thumb. And to show you how dumb I can get, I let my mind kind of dream around about how someday I'd come back all rich and famous and give Florence and Ernest a lot of money and they'd be happy and love me for it. . . .

Just pictures in my mind those things were, but they seemed real, as I was standing alongside the road in the May morning, and they made me feel good about running off, which maybe wasn't such a good thing to do.

Maybe because I was daydreaming I missed the first three cars that went by, and I started worrying that I'd stand there all day and that Florence and Ernest would come home and catch me before I was even gone.

That thought made me perk up. The next rig that came by was a truck full of hogs, and I splattered a smile across my face and tried to look friendly, and the truck stopped.

Funny, but looking back, it seems like somebody was trying to tell me something about what was going to happen to me, because the hog farmer had his whole family in the front of the truck with him. There wasn't any room for me.

"Back there," he said, leaning out the window and

spitting snoose onto the highway. "No room up front. Sorry."

I thanked him anyway, because he *did* stop, and climbed into the open rack of the back of the truck with twenty-eight full-sized Yorkshire brood sows that didn't like riding in the truck.

It was already toe deep back there, and naturally the farmer jerked the clutch when he took off, so I wasn't ready and fell down and got it on my hands and knees, and nothing, nothing in the whole world smells like pig dirt.

That farmer took me just under ninety miles without stopping, at about forty miles an hour, and I don't want to seem ungrateful, but there were times when I would have paid him to stop and let me off, or just to slow down so I could jump for it.

But he didn't even slow down, didn't hear me yelling back there, and when he finally pulled off the highway and stopped so I could get out, I was so ripe, flies wouldn't land on me.

He drove off before I could thank him, which was probably just as well, considering the mood I was in, and I found myself standing in the middle of North Dakota at noon smelling like the bottom of a pig barn.

And that might not be the worst start for somebody going off to seek fame and fortune, but I've never heard of a poorer one.

★ 2 ★

There was some water in the ditch by the highway, and I cleaned my hands and tried to get the stains out of my knees. But the stink was still there, so strong I couldn't see getting a ride in anything but another pig truck. Somebody might stop, but they'd never let me in a car unless they couldn't smell.

Still, ninety miles wasn't far enough for a good runoff. I had to get some distance between me and home, or they'd catch me right away. So I started hoofing it, heading west down the highway, and as luck would have it a pickup came along and stopped even though I didn't have my thumb out.

It was a brand-new half ton. The guy sitting at the wheel wore a cowboy hat, and he was about twenty or so. There were some ropes hanging from the gun rack in the back window of the cab.

"Climb in," he said, when I got to the door. "I'll take you down a piece."

"Maybe I should ride in back," I said, watching his face when the smell got to him. "I rode in a pig truck."

"Ahh, bull, get in. We'll keep the windows down. I gotta have somebody to talk to or I'll fall asleep. Been on the road eighteen hours."

I threw my suitcase in back and got into the truck. It was a little close, but not too bad with the windows rolled down and the wind-wings wide open so the air moved through a lot.

"You riding chuck?" he asked, when we were back on the road and moving.

"Pardon?" I didn't know what he meant.

"You on the bum—riding chuck, looking for a bunk, a job?" He shot me a glance like maybe my education had been slow. "Looking for work?"

"Oh. Yeah. Going out to work the sugar-beet farms." I tried to sound like I knew what I was talking about. "I do it every year—to make money for school."

I was a little worried that he'd find out I was a runaway and turn me in, but it was a stupid thing to worry about. I was the last thing on his mind except for my ears. When he said he wanted somebody to talk to he wasn't kidding.

"Reminds me of when I was young," he started. "Working oil rigs down in dust country—Okie land. Oklahoma. Whooeee! I cut some high cotton down there, I'll tell the *world*. . . . "

Figuring he was only twenty, maybe three or four years older than I was, he must have crammed a pile of traveling into his life. Going like a machine, he told me about the oil fields, working in California, riding the circuit up in Canada—the rodeo circuit— and just a whole mess of places and things he just couldn't have seen or done, so it didn't take me long to figure he was lying.

But it was all right. It was the kind of lying that didn't hurt anybody, the kind he didn't expect anybody to believe anyway.

I quit listening when he started a story about a girl in Texas he'd met while he was working a spread down there. It was an all-right story, and the way he described the girl was interesting, but I'd heard the story before when Freddy Haldine told it as a joke in the locker room in gym, and it wasn't the kind of joke you needed to hear twice.

I laughed when he got to the part where the girl plugged in the electric fence, and after that I just nodded and smiled where I was supposed to and stared out the window at North Dakota and felt blue.

Well, not blue exactly, but choked up a little in my mind, like you get in the thick part of a movie. I guess I was feeling a little sorry for myself.

Like when we'd pass a farm, tucked in and neat, in between green fields of beet tops or thick winter wheat, all I could think of was how nice it would be to live there. Not just be there, but *belong* there so it was home.

Funny, but now that I think of it that feeling got stronger the farther I got from home—got so it was part of me. And even later, with Tiltawhirl and the carnival, I'd catch myself looking at farms that way. It was worse at night, when you were out in the dark and the lights came from the house all cheery and warm-yellow.

"What's the matter, boy?" the cowboy yelled over

the roar of the wind through the windows. "Sleep got to you?"

I shook my head. Somehow I'd closed my eyes without meaning to. "No. I'm listening. Go ahead."

"Well, I was just going to tell you about this rodeo down in Montrose, Colorado," he said, shifting his mouth back into second. "We was drawing for bulls—I rode bulls before I got busted up—and I pulled an old widowmaker named Turbine. . ."

Some of his stories were true, but not true for him. He'd use stories other people had told him and just put his own name in, and that was all right because the story was still good even if the names were changed.

Like I knew he was too young and green to have been busted up by bulls riding the rodeo. But there was so much good in the story—about the bull stomping the clown and ripping up the stands—that it was fun to listen to anyway, and interesting if I picked out the true parts and let the bushwa slide past.

We drove like that for three hours, kind of in a southwestern direction across the state, and he must have been doing at least seventy because the engine was a whine all the way.

From what he said he was going all the way across North Dakota and into Wyoming, and he wouldn't mind company all the way. But I'd been watching the fields, and the farther west we got, the more sugar beets there were—just miles and miles of green rows. And there were people working in the fields, hunched over, so when I finally saw a sign that said "Farm Workers Wanted," I asked him to pull over.

"Here?" He pointed out at the fields. "Ain't nothing here but beets and sky."

"Here." I nodded, and he swung the truck over to the shoulder and stopped. I climbed out and grabbed my suitcase from the back. "Thanks—thanks a lot. I hope you have good luck at the rodeos."

"Shoot, boy, ain't you going to shake hands?"

I shrugged and reached in and shook, and when I pulled my hand back there was a twenty-dollar bill in it.

"Hey! I don't need this."

"Buy food," he yelled, shifting the truck and starting away. "Eat up before you work—ain't nothing to you."

And he drove off, the truck whining into high and the wheels making a wet-slick sound as he got up to speed. It was late afternoon, coming on evening, and I watched the truck until it disappeared in the heat shimmer off the highway.

I don't know why, but he was like a friend leaving me, and it was strange because I didn't even know his name—just that he told good stories, even if they weren't true.

Of course I didn't know it, but those stories would be the only thing keeping my mind straight in the next month when everything turned upside down and backward so that even meeting somebody like Tiltawhirl John, even somebody as grunt-rough as T-John, would be nice.

I didn't know any of that when I picked up my suitcase and went down the driveway with the sign.

All I knew was they wanted farm workers, and it was a start at getting rich and famous. And that's

what I was thinking when I walked down the driveway and started the old collie barking at the Singletree Beet Farm just outside of Jefferson, North
Dakota.

★ 3 ★

It seems to me that we're all messed up when it comes to knowing good or bad people by the way they look. Maybe it's because of the movies, and how the bad guys always look uglier than John Wayne, or maybe it's just that we *want* bad people to be ugly so we can hate them easier.

I don't know why, but I'm almost always wrong when I look at somebody and try to decide whether he's good or bad.

Back in town there's this guy who's old and he has a hunchback and he lives in a hut in back of the saloon and drinks cheap wine. I *wanted* him to be mean because he is the ugliest thing I've ever seen.

Well, don't you know that inside he's the sweetest and most beautiful person in the world. He spends all his time writing songs, until he gets drunk and passes out, and taking care of stray cats and dogs.

And those songs he writes are all about soft and beautiful things, which I know because I heard him singing one night while I was waiting for my uncle to come out of the bar.

His name is Milt—Milton Van Sickle—and when he dies it's going to be sad not just for the dogs and cats, but for all of us, because his songs will be gone.

But like I said, when I first saw old Milt I wanted him to be mean because he was so ugly. The same thing, only opposite, happened when I met Karl Elsner, who was head of the Singletree Beet Farm.

When I walked down the driveway the dog started barking, and this big man came out of the house. He stood over six feet, built heavy and round, and he was all blond—even his eyebrows. He looked so jolly he could have been a giant Santa Claus. He was just all smiles, and I *knew* he was good the minute I saw him, just by looking at him.

"Hello, boy," he said, smiling, when I came into the yard around the big white farmhouse. "Can I help you?"

So I told him my name, and lied about working for school money, and told him I'd seen his sign and wanted a job.

"Well, now," he said, looking me up and down. There was a little gravy on his shirt. He'd just come from eating, and the gravy was on his belly—just at my eye level. "You ever work a hoe?"

"Yes, sir." I lied. "Last year."

"Where was that?"

"Back east a bit—around Grafton."

He studied me for a moment. "You don't look big enough for a hoe."

"I'm wiry," I said, which was partially true. "And I work hard."

He nodded, but the smile was gone. "Can you work from can to can't?"

"What do you mean?"

"Just that, boy. I pay twelve dollars an acre for thinning beets, every other one, and I only pay if you work from can to can't—from dawn to dark and then some, until you can't see."

I nodded. "Yes, I can—from can to can't."

"Then we'll put you on a hoe and see. Have you eaten?"

I started to lie again, to tell him that I'd just had a bite, but my stomach was kissing my backbone, it was so empty. "I'd like a sandwich or something," I said. "Not a whole meal."

"Wait here." He went into the house and came out a minute later with a big bowlful of stew and gravy, and two chunks of bread for sopping. "Eat this, then go to the barn. You'll sleep there tonight, and tomorrow I'll put you in with the rest of the workers. It's too late now—don't want to disturb them."

I wondered why it was too late, being just soft dark, but the stew was awfully good and it didn't seem the time to ask questions. Then, too, he seemed so nice—so open and friendly—that it didn't feel right to get pushy or wise.

I knocked off the stew straight away, then he took me to the barn and showed me the feed room. It was filled with sacks, empty and full of mash for the cows, and he handed me ten or fifteen empty sacks.

"Make a bed and curl down," he said. "Morning

comes fast and I don't waste daylight. Breakfast is ten minutes after I ring the bell."

I nodded.

"Tomorrow night you'll sleep with the other workers, like I said, but for tonight you stay in here. Don't go wandering around the farm." On that last his voice got serious, and I looked up at him, let my eyes ask.

"The dog," he said. "After dark he goes mean. It's not good to be around the yard then. He might go for you."

"Oh. Well, I'm too tired to move anyway."

He nodded and turned to go. "Tomorrow night you'll know what tired means."

Then he left me alone, and I made a bed out of the sacks. It itched some, but not too much. I knew the itch wouldn't bother me near as much as the smell of pig that still came from my clothes.

There was an overhead light in the room, a bare bulb, and I jerked the cord when I got my bed made. Then I lay back in the dark and thought about the day, let it come in on me like sleep.

It seemed like years since I'd left home, and it had just been this morning. I worked at that for a while, wondering how time could change so much.

Time got me to thinking about how long I'd been gone, and that got me to thinking about money— fame and fortune. And I wondered how long it would take to hoe an acre of sugar beets, figuring that even if you only got one acre a day done you could get rich in nothing flat. Twelve dollars a day was a pile of money.

Pretty soon it all rolled into one lump—the money

and the cowboy telling stories in the truck and the warm stew in my belly—and I dropped off to sleep so heavy even the smell of pig didn't bother me.

Only no sooner was I asleep than the dreams came. They were nightmares, and what made them strange was that they were in a language I couldn't understand.

I dreamed I was asleep in a strange place, surrounded by something warm, and these strange voices started yelling in a language I didn't know but had heard before.

They were angry yells, somewhere outside my dream, so I couldn't see where they were coming from—wild cries.

Then this deep voice yelled in English, hard and loud, "Get back in there, you stinking greaser." That was followed by a loud *chunk* sound like somebody dropping a watermelon on cement, and right then I woke up, looking around.

But it was quiet in the feed room—so quiet that when I strained to listen all I heard was my own breathing—and in a little time I went back to sleep.

And this time I dreamed—only it wasn't a nightmare. It was about girls and a time when I'd gone to a movie with one. When I'd walked her home from the movie I'd kissed her, and that was in the dream, but there was more, too, which I'd rather not go into, because it was the sort of dream that made you not want to get up in the morning even if you stood to make twelve dollars a day hoeing sugar beets.

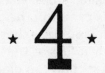

★ 4 ★

There wasn't any light coming through the little window in the feed room when the bell started ringing. I tumbled out of the sacks and went outside to the gray of early morning.

The bell stopped when I hit the outside, and I stood for a minute or so getting my bearings. The truth of it was that I wasn't really awake yet and didn't know where I was. I was still thinking about the dream.

Then it came back to me, and I saw some people about a hundred yards away, making for some tables under a big tarp. It figured that was the chow hall, so I made for it, and when I got closer I could see that the people were all Mexicans. They were wearing those little white outfits you see in movies all the time, and straw hats with the tassle, and as I approached two or three of them looked up but didn't say anything.

"Hi." I tried it, but got no answer, so I gave it up. If they didn't want to talk to me, that was their business. I was here to hoe beets and get rich, not to make friends.

I slid into the bench bolted to the table and sat down. There was a tin plate already there, with a spoon, and I figured that was really service until I noticed that the plate was nailed down to the table and hadn't been washed since God made dirt. There was a quarter inch of grease in the bottom, and when I looked at the spoon I could see that it was chained to the table with about a foot of that bathtub-stopper chain and was dirtier than the plate.

Still, I've never been one to make waves, and if that was the way they ate around there I'd just have to go with it—no sense embarrassing anybody. I tried to get a little grease out of the plate with my shirt elbow, doing it so nobody would notice, and wiped the spoon on my pants leg.

By this time the sky was starting to lighten, and I could see the people sitting around me a little better.

Funny thing—they didn't make any sound. There were women and kids there, along with the men, all sitting at those nailed-down plates, and even the kids were silent. Not a whisper.

It was frankly kind of spooky, and I was on the edge of getting the jim-jams when the owner, Karl (I found out his name later when I came to hate him), came out of the big house with a huge pot of beans and a sackful of bread slices.

"Good morning!" he boomed, and he laughed as he came under the tarp. "Good day for thinning—warm and dry. Good day."

I threw him a smile, but I could see that the others at the table didn't, which seemed sour since he was being so nice.

"You ready for work, boy?" he asked me, all happy and loud. "Ready for two thousand acres of beets?"

I nodded, and a picture flashed through my mind—all numbers. Two thousand acres of beets he had, at twelve dollars an acre. That was twenty-four thousand dollars. More money than there was in the whole world.

"Eat heavy," he said, putting the pot and bag on the table, "because there's no lunch."

He turned away, and I filled my plate when the pot came by. They were pinto beans—just beans with nothing else in them except for the juice—and the bread was old and dry.

But it was food and I was hungry, and I even forgot the dirty spoon and plate while I shoveled it down, sopping the bread in the bean juice to soften it. That bread was as hard as a rock.

Fast as I ate, the rest ate faster, and I saw why when Karl pulled up in a big stake-bed truck. The beans hadn't been on the table for ten minutes, maybe only five, and he was ready to take us out to the fields.

"Off and on," he yelled, "off and on. Let's go. We're wasting daylight."

I got up and followed the others, carrying a piece of bread with beans on it, and climbed into the truck. By now it was full light, with the sun coming over the eastern edge of things, and I could see a barrelfull of hoes in the front of the truck. I got up front by the barrel and hunkered into the corner so I was braced on both sides.

The rest of them piled in beside me, still silent, and we drove out to the fields, which were only about half a mile from the house.

Karl stopped the truck on the edge of the road, so he wouldn't have to drive in the beets, and we got out. I saw the rest of them grabbing hoes when they got out, so I did the same, and was surprised to find that most of the hoe handle had been sawed off. They were only about three feet long.

"Hey, you got any longer-handled hoes?" I asked Karl, who'd gotten out of the truck and walked around to the back. "Mine's sawed off."

"They all are," he said, smiling. "That's to keep you from leaning on them. Can't have you going to sleep on the hoe."

Of course I thought he was ragging me, thought they were probably sawed off to make working them easier, so I didn't say anything.

"Over here." He motioned for me to follow him, though I could see the rest of them go off and start working because he'd already shown them how to do it when they first came.

I stopped next to him, and he pointed down at the row of beets.

"We overplant to make sure we get a good crop," he said, using his boot toe to scruffle the top of a plant, which looked just like a turnip or rutabaga. "Now, when they're young, we have to go through and cut out every other one to allow the good ones to grow."

He took the hoe from me and cut the tops off a couple plants. "See? You hit one, miss the next, and hit the next. It's that simple. Got it?"

I nodded. "Sure—no sweat." I took the hoe and chopped a couple to show him I knew what he was talking about.

"Fine. You're on your own, boy."

"Wait, before you go—how much is an acre?" I pointed at the field. "How will I know when I get an acre done?"

He laughed. "You'll know, boy, you'll know. Way it works in this field, when you get two rows done the full length of the field, you'll have an acre done."

Then he drove off, and I turned and looked at the rows of beets.

They went out of sight. They went for a week and a Sunday, those rows, until they were lost in the morning mist, which was the dew cooking off the plants as the sun came up high enough to hit the leaves.

I couldn't believe how long the rows of beets were, or that it would take two of them to make an acre, but even as I stood looking at them I could see that the Mexicans had already started.

I watched them for a minute to see how they did it. All of them, even the women and kids, were working, and some of the bigger men were using two hoes at the same time, chopping left and right and left and right, like machines, working two rows at the same time.

It made me think of the story of John Henry driving railroad spikes as I watched them working all hunched over and quiet, just *whack* and *whack*. They even looked kind of pretty, their white suits against the green of the beet crops—pretty like some paintings I'd seen in a book.

But looking at them wasn't getting my rows hoed, wasn't getting me rich—although after seeing how long the rows were I was having second thoughts about that fame-and-fortune business—at least as far as hoeing sugar beets was concerned.

So I hunched over the way they were doing, and got the hoe going, and pretty soon there wasn't anything in the world but the sun on my back and the beet tops falling over as the hoe cut through the rich green leaves on top of the plant—just *whack* and *whack,* and the thick juice of the beets smearing the hoe all shiny and green.

⋆ 5 ⋆

I found out two things before noon and I've never forgotten them.

Hoeing sugar beets is the most boring work in the whole world. It's worse than watching grass grow—so stupid and dumb and boring that pretty soon you forget what you're doing, and the work takes over and your mind goes away while you chop without thinking. You get into this rhythm where you hoe and step, and hoe and step, and it doesn't take long before you don't even see the beets anymore. Your eyes glaze over and the sun cooks you and it's like you've never done anything else in your life but hoe beets, never been anywhere but in the beet fields.

The other thing I learned was that Karl Elsner was mean. No, he was *evil*, because his smile made you think he was all right, only the truth was that the smile didn't mean anything; it was just there, like his suntan. Or maybe I should say his sunred, because he didn't really get tan so much as burned.

I would have found out that night anyway, which I'll talk about in a minute, but something happened in the beet field just before noon, and I got my first good look at what evil can be when it's in a man like Karl Elsner.

I worked fast, but even so, the Mexicans pulled away from me—whether because they'd had practice or were stronger or just faster, I couldn't say. Probably all three.

But as we came onto noon—and by this time I could see that there was no way I'd make an acre a day, that I'd be lucky to get half an acre, six dollars' worth—as we worked into noon, I noticed that one of the Mexicans, an older man, who was maybe forty or forty-five, seemed to be dropping back from the rest of them, the sweep of his hoe slowing down.

Well, I thought, at least I'm as good as one of them when it comes down to the stretch. I know how that sounds, what my grandma used to call miffy or a kind of selfish mad, but I was hurting some. I wanted to be as good as they were, and I can't explain it except to say that I felt sort of as if I didn't belong and that working as fast and good as they did would make me feel closer to them.

Anyway, I was chopping away when I saw this old guy falling back. He was still working his hoe, but he was going slower and slower, and pretty soon I was alongside him.

Well, right away I made a kind of race out of it. And that was just about as stupid and dumb as it sounds, but I did it, whipped my hoe faster and faster and went on by him and felt good inside for doing it. Later I wished I hadn't felt good that way, hadn't felt so proud for passing the old man. But that's how I felt at the time.

When I got past him I eased off and took a sneaky look kind of back under my armpit, and I saw the old man stop.

Just like that. He didn't fall over, or stand up. He just stopped, with his hoe halfway through a plant top and his back hunched over and his hands all leathery and shining on the wood of the hoe handle. I swear he looked like a statue. He looked like a statue carved of fine wood that had been put there in the middle of the field, he was so still.

I started to hoe again, but when he didn't move I stopped and turned.

"You all right?" I stood up from my crouch, feeling the muscles in my back pulling. I mean I *hurt*.

He didn't answer, didn't even look up, but just stood like that, still and staring down at the dirt. It was creepy.

I put my hoe down, noticing for the first time that my hands were cramped around the handle like two claws, and looked at him for a full thirty seconds.

For that long he didn't move, and I thought maybe he'd died, that his heart had stopped. I'd heard of it happening, people just dying like that.

Then it seemed that the handle of the hoe was collapsing as he slid down to the ground. He just slid down and down until his face nestled into the dirt in between the rows of beets.

I started to move then, back toward him, but I hadn't gone four steps when a woman came by me and said something in Spanish that I couldn't understand but could tell wasn't very nice by the tone of her voice. I didn't know if she was mad at me or just at the world or what, and I hurried to follow her to the old man.

She knelt down in the dirt and pulled his head into her lap and said soft words that were more like music, and petted him on the temples. It was then, when she turned his head over, that I saw the marks. I hadn't noticed them in the dark of the breakfast tent, and later, on the truck, I'd been looking at the hoes in the barrel. Besides, there had been other people packed around me.

But now I could see them—long, ugly black marks on the sides of his head and down on his neck where his loose shirt didn't cover him.

He'd been beaten. Not just tapped or shoved around, but beaten hard, the kind of beating that hurts deep and long and sometimes kills. I'd only seen it once before, when two guys fought over a woman in a parking lot by the bar back in town. They'd fought with clubs made of two-by-fours and they'd both wound up in the hospital.

"God," I said, not swearing but because that's what came to mind. "He was hoeing and all the time he was like that. What happened . . . ? "

It started out as a question, but I didn't finish it because the night before had come back into my mind like a train.

The dream. Only it hadn't been a dream, it had been real. Somebody in the yard had been doing this to the old man—beating the peewadden out of him, hurting him inside.

"But *why*?" I knelt down beside the woman, but she pushed me away.

"*Gringo!*" She said it like she would say spit, and I think she would have hit me if she hadn't been holding the old man.

"I was just trying to help." I settled back on my haunches. "He needs help." Dumb, but I've always been like that; just say what comes to mind when things get tight. Sometimes it helps, usually it doesn't, but I do it anyway. "He needs help bad."

"My daughter," the old man whispered, his eyes open, "she doesn't speak English. Doesn't understand that you want to help."

Then he whispered something to her in Spanish, and she gave me a quick look that was still mad but not as hot as before.

"What happened? Who beat you like that?" I tried to keep my eyes off the marks, because it isn't nice to stare, but I couldn't—they were so *black*. Like paint on his brown skin. "Who worked you over?"

He smiled. I swear to God, he smiled, and it came out sad from his eyes. "Does it matter? It's just a beating; it will pass."

I could have argued that, not knowing how tough he was, but I didn't say anything about it. If he didn't want to tell me who'd worked him up like that he didn't have to. It might have been one of the others, or anybody.

But the girl got the drift of what we were talking about, and she looked up at me and pointed at the marks and said:

"Karl Elsner—*el patrón*."

"You mean the owner did this?" I couldn't believe it. "The big guy?"

"That is right." The old man sighed. "She is still young enough to hold anger. It was the owner. And you must run, you must leave this farm now, while you have the chance. It is one of the bad ones. You must leave."

"Why don't you?" It came out kind of smart sounding, but I didn't mean it that way. "Why do you stay?"

"Because we must. We cannot leave until the beets are done, until he doesn't need us anymore. But you don't have to stay. You can leave, and you must."

And just for the record I thought it over, thought it over while I knelt in the dirt next to the old man and his daughter, with the noon sun down on us. I thought it over and decided not to leave.

I'd like to say it was because I wanted to help them, or find out what was happening, and maybe there *was* a little of that in my mind. But mostly I didn't believe it, couldn't believe that the big smiling man could have done this terrible thing to the old man, beat him this way. I just couldn't make it stick in my skull, even with him down right in front of me so I could see the marks.

And that's why I stayed, at least for the first day.

And by the second day it didn't matter, because then I was in the trap and couldn't leave, even though I wanted to more than anything else in the world. And after that it just got worse and worse until my mind tipped over and I met T-John.

★ **6** ★

After a time the old man got up and, thinking back, I don't see how he did it. I couldn't have gotten up, and how he did it at his age is beyond me. What's more, he worked, not fast, but he worked, and between watching him hoe and taking care of my own rows, the afternoon passed like nothing.

Soon it was evening, and we'd worked all day without food or water. Then it was coming on dark with a mist in the air and the coolness coming out of the ground, and finally, when it was almost hard dark, Elsner came driving up in the truck.

We climbed in and went back to the farm headquarters and had beans and dried bread for supper, with some coffee that was almost cold.

I'd worked from can to can't. I was so tired I could hardly walk, and there were muscles in my back and arms that had taken a set, so I couldn't straighten up or stretch my arms. My hands were blisters all over, and some of them had broken and bled. I don't want to go on about myself but that's how it was; hoeing beets is murder, murder slowed down just a little.

When we had finished eating, the Mexicans got up and headed out for some small huts south of the barn, and I headed for the feed room.

"Where you going, boy?" Elsner came out of the big house and stood under the yard light so I could see him. He was smiling. "You sleep with the others from now on, all right?"

It seemed that he was asking, but not really, because in back of the smile, down in his voice, there was something hard, like gravel in meat, hidden but there.

I turned and followed the Mexicans, too tired to say anything, and right away I had a problem. I didn't know where to bunk down. They were all kind of splitting up and going to different huts, and I couldn't see how I could just barge in and say "I'm sleeping here" without cutting in on someone's privacy.

"You may sleep with us," the old man called off to the left as if he'd read my mind. "We have room."

"Thanks." I said it out loud, but I don't think it was more than a whisper. Along with everything else, working in the sun all day without water had made me hoarse. "Thanks a lot."

He and the girl, who I found later was named Maria and who was just over sixteen, but older because of her life, if you know what I mean, went into the shack on the end of the row, and I stopped on the step outside.

Fumbling-around sounds came from inside the

hut, and pretty soon a match flared and a yellow glow came out of the doorway from an oil lamp.

In the light from the lamp I could make out the inside of the shack, and there wasn't much to see. The lamp was on a table in the middle of the one room, which was only about ten by ten feet, and that was it. Some old army blankets were spread around on the floor, and over in the corner was a cream can.

"Come in," the old man said, settling down on one of the blankets. "*Mi casa, su casa*." And he laughed, but there wasn't anything funny in it, just tired and sad. I found out later that what he'd said meant, My house is your house, which is a kind of nice saying, but in this case didn't mean anything because he was making a sad joke out of the shack.

I went in and kind of staggered over to a blanket in a corner. There weren't any pillows or padding under the blankets, just the rough wood floor, but it still felt nice to settle back against the wall and let the pain go out.

"You are learning about beets." The old man's voice was ragged. "What it is like to know beets."

It wasn't really a question, but I nodded. My eyes were closed, but I heard movement and opened them to see Maria dip a corner of a blanket in the cream can and bring it out wet with water. She knelt down beside the old man and began bathing his bruises. There was anger in her movements, all tight and quick, but her touch was soft, and he smiled.

"For years I have worked the beets." He winced when the cold water touched a tender spot. "Many, many times have I come across the river in the dark and ridden the buses north on the roads where nobody watches to work the beets. And now Maria comes, because her mother couldn't. . . . "

I was listening, but it was like his voice was covered with dust or something. The words seemed to be under something, so I could just hear them, and it took me a moment to figure that it was just me being tired.

"In all that time this is only the third bad *patrón* I have seen." He sighed. "This Karl Elsner, he is the worst."

"Did he really beat you? Was it really him?" I still couldn't believe it.

He nodded. "As he would beat you, if you left the shack tonight. He is out there, waiting. He is out there every night." He said it as if he were talking about a monster. "Every night, watching."

I thought about checking it out, but to be honest I was so tired I couldn't move, didn't really care. "Why do you stay?"

"Because we are here illegally. We came across the river in the night. If we make trouble he will turn us in. And there are many others up here working for good *patrones*. They, too, would have to go back, or maybe to jail. So we must stay and not make trouble. . . ."

His voice slowed down, and I opened my eyes, thinking he was asleep, but he wasn't.

" . . . we are like the beets that must be thinned so the others can grow fat. Like the beets."

This time he stopped, and Maria let him lie back on the blanket, lowered him softly down, like a baby.

Then she got up and blew the lamp out. In a moment I could hear water splashing, and I knew she was washing herself back in the corner, taking a quick bath. Normally I would have tried to take a look, because she wasn't at all ugly and was fairly big where it counts, but I was too tired, and something else was mixing with the tired. A thought kept coming through.

I couldn't leave either. I was in a trap, just like the old man and the rest of them.

I was there illegally. I was a runaway, and if I made trouble or tried to take off, Elsner would call the law in, and all those people working for the good ranchers would lose their jobs.

And maybe that didn't make a lot of sense, but I was tired and not thinking too straight, and that's how it came out.

I had to stay, just like the rest of them. I was trapped and had to stay and hoe beets and eat beans and dried bread that Elsner probably got from the garbage cans of a bakery. And the only thing that made any of it worth doing was that I'd done half an acre of beets.

Half an acre the first day, six dollars. Maybe it wasn't much, but it was something and I'd get better. In a few days I'd be doing almost an acre a day, when the blisters turned to leather and my back muscles got stronger.

Twelve dollars a day, I thought, letting the curtain down over my brain and going to sleep. I'd be making twelve dollars a day, and that made up for a lot of beans and dried bread.

And just for the record, to show you how dumb a guy can be, I actually thought that, mean as Elsner was, as rotten as he fed us, he intended to pay.

Maybe it's part of growing up, where you go through a phase and want to believe what you want to believe even when it isn't true. Because that's what I was doing.

I think I knew then that Elsner wasn't going to pay, ever, but I wanted to believe he would, and so that's what I did. I just made it up in my mind that we'd all get rich.

I fell asleep counting money.

★ 7 ★

And it went like that for a week, just working and sleeping and working, and then it went on for another week.

Looking back, it seems strange that it could happen, that I could just work like that and eat beans and dried bread and that nothing else would happen, not even talk. But that's the way it was, and you'd have to hoe beets to understand how it can happen.

It's not like other farm work—not like picking or plowing or combining. In all those other kinds of work there's variety; things change, or there are other people right around you, and you talk and maybe laugh.

When you hoe beets you're alone, so alone you might as well be on another planet. There are other people in the field, sure, but everybody works at his own speed, and that scatters people around so usually nobody is close to you.

And when you hoe beets and work from can to can't you don't talk at night or in the morning, even if you're happy, which we weren't. You get too tired, always too tired. Even when I hardened a bit and got stronger, so I was making almost an acre a day, I was still so shot when we got done at night that I could only eat and sleep. We never talked again in the hut the way we did the first night; we just came in and dropped—except for Maria, of course, who always washed, but whom I never really saw.

And finally, when you hoe beets nothing changes, not ever. That's boring, but it's more, too, because you don't see the end of the work and can't remember the beginning. The only thing that counts is sliding that hoe back and forth to cut off the beet tops. You forget everything else.

Like I forgot the sky. It was in the second week that it hit me that I hadn't looked at the sky in days, hadn't looked up even when I wasn't hoeing. And that scared me. I thought I was going crazy, and after that I made a point of looking up once in a while just to make sure it was there.

And it was in that second week that I forgot what that girl I'd kissed once looked like—couldn't picture her to save my soul. I tried hard, too, and when nothing came I dug around for other things to remember to keep my mind from going, and I came up with the stories the cowboy had told me in the pickup. They stuck, for some reason, and I worked them back and forth in my mind the way I'd slide Jello around in my mouth to enjoy the cool feel and taste of it—just to remember something, just to *know* something besides beets.

I guess you turn into a kind of animal when you work like that, or maybe a robot. And it wasn't just me, either. The rest of them were the same.

It was in that second week that I was working in back of Maria, behind her. She was about five hundred yards ahead of me and two rows over, and it was afternoon and hot and I was really into the rhythm of it, just hoe and step, and hoe and step, when I almost stepped on a rattlesnake.

He was about three feet long and squirming across the row right in front of me, and I almost wet myself when I saw him.

Then I noticed that his head was cut off, clean as a whistle, so there was only the stump. He had rolled onto his back so his pale-yellow belly showed in the sun, and the stump where his head used to be was striking at my hoe and the beet plants around him.

I looked up ahead at Maria, and I thought, How could that be? How could it be that a girl-woman could just hoe beets and come on a rattlesnake and cut off his head without saying anything, without breaking her stride?

She'd thinned the snake, just like another beet top, flicked his head off without saying a word or making a sound, and gone on down the row.

The snake was just another beet, and I felt a chill go down my back watching it rolling over and squirming as if it were looking for its head. If you can do that to a snake, I thought, you can do it to anything, even to a person.

Nothing matters but the beets when you're hoeing, nothing.

And that's why I could work, just work, for two

weeks and then a third one and not do anything else, not even talk at night, just eat and work and sleep. I lost count of how much I'd hoed, couldn't keep track, and so I took to making a mark on my hoe handle every time I'd finished an acre, and by the end of the third week I had sixteen marks.

Sixteen acres at twelve dollars an acre. One hundred and ninety-two dollars in three weeks—that's how I saw it, and that thought kept me going, even though I kind of sensed that I would never get any money.

In the middle of the fourth week, after I'd been almost a month at the farm, there came a rain in the middle of the morning, and if I ever get a chance, I'd like to talk to whoever made that rain. If it had just come two weeks sooner, I wouldn't have been out so much work. . . .

But it came in the morning in the middle of the fourth week, and it poured so hard that we couldn't work. The fields were just mud, mud up to your ankles, and even Elsner could tell that we'd do more damage than good if we kept working, by tearing the plants out.

It was funny, the way the rain hit us. We started working at dawn, and at about nine or ten the rain came and everybody stopped. Right where we were, we stopped, when the mud got bad, and for a minute we just stood and felt lost.

We couldn't hoe, and there didn't seem to be anything else in the whole world *but* hoeing, so we just stood, just stopped, like machines that had run out of gas, and felt the rain soak into our clothes.

In thirty minutes or so Elsner came from wherever

it was he went with the truck every day. We loaded in, and he took us back to the farm, and that was the first time in almost a month that we had a time when we weren't working or sleeping.

You get used to things, even misery like hoeing beets, and it felt strange to go to the huts when it was still daylight. For a few minutes we followed our old habits. I went into the hut in back of Maria and the old man and got on my blanket in the corner and had even started to go to sleep when it hit me that it wasn't noon yet and we had a whole day to play around.

That's when I decided to go collect my pay for what I'd done so far. I told the old man about it, and he said something in Spanish to Maria and they both laughed.

"*Loco*." Maria pointed at me and then made a sign by her temple to show I was crazy. "*Muy loco*."

"She says you are crazy," the old man said. "Very crazy to think you will be paid for your work. Why should he pay when he doesn't need to?"

"Still." I stood up. "With all of it, he should still pay."

They both laughed when I left the hut and went to the truck for my hoe, which was in the barrel, so I could count the marks and know how much money he owed me.

I found Elsner by the barn, working on a tractor. He was changing oil, and he came out from under when I walked up, wiping his hands.

"What can I do you for, boy?" The same smile was plastered across his face.

"I'd like to be paid for what I've done so far," I told

him, holding up the hoe handle so he could see the marks. "Twenty-one and a half acres."

"Well, we usually wait until the job is done before paying."

"If it's all the same, I'd like mine now."

"Sure, sure. If that's the way you want it, that's the way you get it. Let's see, twenty-one and a half acres at twelve dollars an acre . . . "

I helped him out. "It's two hundred and fifty-eight dollars."

"So it is. You're absolutely right."

"Well?"

"Come on up to the house," he said, starting out, "so we can do the final figuring."

So I followed him, although I didn't know what he meant by final figuring when I'd just told him what he owed for my work, and I stood on the back step of the house in the rain because field hands were never allowed in the big house. I wasn't even supposed to be in the main yard or around the buildings.

When you hoe beets you're the bottom.

I stood there for a good long time—over half an
hour—and when he finally came back out his hands
were empty.

"I finished the final figuring," he said, and that
false smile was there, "and we come out even."

"Even?" I thought I'd heard him wrong.

"Yeah. Actually you owe me a little, but you've
been a pretty good worker, so I'll call it even." He
stopped and looked over my shoulder back toward the
huts. Maria had come out of the hut to go to the
outhouse, and her dress was wet, and you could pretty
much see how she was made right through the cloth.

"Now there's one ready for picking," Elsner said,
watching her walk. "She's *ready* for picking."

"What do you mean, *even*?" I changed the subject
back to my money. "I figure you owe me. How do you
come out that we're even?"

"Well, first there's the price of the hoe you're holding. They cost over ten dollars, and the labor to cut the handles off is another two dollars a hoe."

"You mean I have to *buy* the hoe?" I looked down at it, the blade worn off from long use and resharpening; it must have been five or ten years old. "I don't want the thing."

"Then I'll buy it back from you. Of course there's depreciation on it, and I can only give you a couple dollars for it. . . . "

Well, I'm dumb, but I'm not stupid, if you know what I mean. I could see where it was all leading, but I thought I'd play it out and see how he did it. In the back of my mind I was already trying to figure out a way to kill him and get away with it.

"So that still doesn't make us even."

"Well, no, it doesn't. You're right there, boy." He laughed. "You've earned a lot more than that hoe is worth, that's for sure."

"Well?"

"On top of the hoe there's the food. That's two dollars a meal, or about four dollars a day. . . . "

"For slop?" I was so mad parts of my brain were melting; I mean I was *hot*. "You charge four dollars a day for slop hogs wouldn't touch?"

My anger didn't seem to bother him because he just laughed. "Not slop at all, boy. Them's *beans,* good old pinto beans, greaser food, and bread."

"The bread is dry."

"Just to make it chewy, the way they like it, boy."

"And the rest of the money?" I couldn't help it, I had to ask, but I knew.

"Rent. Think those houses are free, boy? They cost money."

"And that makes us even."

"Well, like I said, not quite even, but you've been a good worker and I figured we can call it square."

"You scum-sucking pile of puke." It was the worst thing I could think of to call him, something I heard a guy say once when he was drunk in back of Tony's bar back home. It seemed to fit, and right after I said it I made my first big mistake for the day.

I took the hoe handle and hit him in the jewels as hard as I could. I swear I half lifted him off the ground, and he was as heavy as a bull. It hurt him deep, because he grunted, and it came up from his belly.

But that wasn't my mistake. The mistake came because I didn't get away fast enough after I hit him. One of those ham hands came around and caught me by the back of the shirt and held me until the pain in his groin went down a little.

Then he laughed. "Whooee, boy, you've got some hard bark on you, hitting me when you're no bigger than a smell in a windstorm."

I tried to break loose but couldn't. His hand was like a butcher's hook on the back of my neck.

"Didn't them greasers tell you that you never hit the *patrón*? Didn't they *tell* you that?"

Then he held me off the ground with one hand and used the hoe with the other, and he beat me like I've never heard of anybody being beaten, not even the old man.

He didn't hit my head but once, and that made colors come, but he worked over my body until I heard things crack inside, until my ribs went and my guts ached and even my legs were nothing but two hanging shreds of pain.

Then he beat me some more, and did it over, and I

thought I was dead or dying because I didn't know anything but the pain, and it just thundered up and down my body. When I finally thought he was done he did it once more and then let me drop so I was a pile in the mud with the rain coming down on me, and I didn't care whether I made it or not. Toward the end I would have given him the money to stop; I would have done anything in the world to stop the beating.

When he was done he threw the hoe down on top of me and walked away laughing. I remember the laugh even now, because it wasn't mean, it was just as jolly as Santa Claus, and that made it evil, because it was a lie like no other lie on earth.

I don't know how long I lay out there in the main yard in the mud. Probably half an hour, but it seemed like years, because I couldn't move and thought my back was broken and I would be paralyzed for life.

I cried some, and swore more, and prayed to God for help in killing Elsner, which is a sin, I know, but I couldn't help the thought. And when all the crying and swearing and praying were done I was still there alone for a long time.

Then Maria came out with the old man, and between them they dragged me back to the hut, where Maria wrapped me in a blanket and leaned back against the wall and put my head in her lap and sang songs I couldn't understand—low songs that weren't really music so much as sounds.

And in a little while my brain tipped over, and I wouldn't have known if the world came to an end.

★ 9 ★

Some things from then on are cloudy, like I'd been in fog when I did them, and I can't remember them the way I should.

What I do remember comes through jerky and boiled down, so it's like the skeleton of what really happened, just the bones; the meat isn't there.

It stopped raining in the night, and I can remember hearing Maria and her father talking about me in Spanish. I couldn't understand what they said, but their voices sounded worried, worried that I would die, and it felt nice to have somebody care about me that way.

Then I went under again, and the next time I came up it was daylight and I was alone. I could see light coming through the open doorway and blue sky, and that meant the fields were dry and everybody was out hoeing, even Maria and the old man. I understood being left alone, because it was the practical thing to do and they were practical people. If I was going to die, I would, and being with me wouldn't change it. If I wasn't going to die, I wasn't, and the beets still had to be hoed. Then, when they were done, they could get away from Elsner.

Near my head was a plate of beans—I guess Maria had torn it off the table and nail—and some dry bread. The bread was out of the question, but I tried a mouthful of beans, scooping them up with my hand.

They got about halfway down, hung there for a few seconds, then came up, and I puked like a dog that has eaten bone splinters. Something inside me was messed up, because I could feel things snap which I heaved, and it hurt like blazes.

After a bit I crawled back in the corner on a blanket and curled up and slept some more, and when I came out of it this time it was dark and my head was in Maria's lap.

She was singing again, only this time it wasn't nice but low and whiny, like I'd heard Indian women sing when somebody dies in the movies, and that made me laugh because I guess Maria thought I was dead or close to it.

Of course the laugh never came, it was just a little movement that doubled me up in pain, and I screamed some, but not too much, and went under again, this time only for a few seconds.

When I straightened things out, Maria was smiling and the singing had stopped. She had the corner of a rag over my mouth, and it had been soaked in bean juice and she let it drip through my lips. I swear those people use bean juice to cure anything, and it must work because I could feel it going down and it was like salve on my insides.

"We thought you were dead." The old man was sitting on the other side. "You didn't breathe that we could see and there was no movement, and so Maria sang the death song from the hills where we live in Chihuahua."

"Thanks." And I meant it, too. I wasn't going to die, I knew that now, could feel it. But when I do go I want somebody to sing like that and grease me through. I was going to say more, but the words got caught on pain.

"It is good that you did not die. We would have been blamed." He snorted, and I could tell now that he was almost shaking with anger—you could feel the heat coming off him. "The *patrón,* the great beater of boys and old men, would have blamed us, and we would be put in prison for killing you. It is always the way."

Maria rattled off some Spanish, and he nodded. "We must go to sleep now. It is late and you need rest, and we have worked the beets."

Maria lay my head back down on a folded blanket, and they moved off and lay down in their own beds.

I'd been sleeping on and off for a whole day and night and was about to explode, which is something they never show in movies when the hero gets clobbered and is laid up.

I mean I had to go to the bathroom so bad it was murder. As soon as I heard them breathing regularly I pulled myself over to the doorway and got it done, almost screaming with pain when I moved. Then I crawled back to my blanket and lay panting and thinking about what the old man had said.

It is always the way, he'd said, about being blamed for killing me. I didn't know what he meant, but after a time I guessed that what he was talking about was that being poor always means you're on the bottom. Or something like that.

It wasn't fair, but that was the way it was, and I couldn't accept it. I mean I understand how it can be, how money makes people right or gives them the hammer, but I couldn't make that right in my mind. And I still can't—not the way the old man did, who pretended that what Elsner did was just another part of hoeing beets. And it hit me while I was lying there that you've got to be whipped a long time, maybe for hundreds of years, to make all that just a part of living and not something that makes you mad and want to fight.

For the old man, it was as if Elsner were just part of the weather or something—like rain that kept you from working. I mean he *expected* it, and even though Elsner had beaten him, too, it didn't make him mad so much as put out that he couldn't hoe beets for a day. Couldn't work.

Maybe that's wisdom and comes when you get old, and maybe he's right, I don't know about that. But I do know I don't want any part of it, because it makes Elsner right, somehow, when you just let him be part of it all and don't fight him. And that's why I think I killed him later that night and crawled off through the beet fields, where I became a man on the run and finally met T-John.

Because what Elsner did was wrong—not just beating the old man and me, but what he tried to do to Maria when he thought we were asleep.

It must have been about midnight when I saw him come to the doorway of the hut. Maria and the old man were asleep, but I was awake because, like I said, I'd been sleeping for over a day and I saw him in the moonlight when he came to the door.

He waited a moment, and I watched him, wondering what he was doing, holding my breath, and then he came into the shack and went over to Maria.

He stood over her for a moment, looking down, and then he crouched and put his hand over her mouth and lowered himself on her, and it was freaky because everything was silent, like an old movie without music.

Even when Maria awakened and her eyes were white and frightened in the dark of the shack, it was silent. I guess she didn't scream because it wouldn't do any good, or maybe she felt like the old man that it was just part of it all, part of hoeing beets. But I didn't feel that way. I went crazy, just flashed red in my brain so nothing else mattered—not the beating or the pain. I started to get up, and my hand came down on my hoe handle. It was next to me on the floor where the old man had thrown it when he brought me in.

I grabbed the hoe and stood up. I didn't care about the pain or anything but killing the big puke head—not just hitting, not just hurting him—I wanted to *kill* him. I walked over to where they lay, with Maria kicking and fighting silently, and I raised the hoe and brought it down on his head so hard my teeth jammed together.

He rolled off her and squirmed on the floor, the way the snake had squirmed in the beets, and he goobered at the mouth and wet himself, and I thought he was done for, dead and working on nerves, just like the snake.

Then I ran out of the hut, and I was crying some because of what I'd done and also because Maria hadn't screamed and I loved her a little. I ran and ran through the beets until I hit a fence that flipped me, hindend first, like an upturned applecart.

Then I crawled, and crawled some more, until I'd gone up the side of a ditch and was on a road, and I kept crawling and crying and puking until headlights came down on me and I heard brakes squealing and that's when I met Tiltawhirl John.

★ 10 ★

"Ahh, ain't nothin' but a kid."

"Yeah. But look at him. He looks like somebody took a tent iron to him. He's been beat on, beat on bad."

"Put him on the side and let's get out of here. He's somebody's kid, and that's trouble for carnies. Dump him and let's make it."

I was still on my hands and knees in the middle of the road and I wasn't thinking too well. The headlights from the truck—I found later it was a big stakebed—were blinding me. All I could hear were voices, two of them men and one woman.

"Kid, kid, can you hear me?" It was the woman's voice and she was kneeling beside me. "Can you understand what I'm saying?"

I nodded but couldn't get any words out. It came to me that I must have been a sight, what with my clothes half torn off and the lumps and puke and all, and I started laughing. Not because it was funny but because I couldn't keep from doing it.

"Easy, kid, easy. Now, you from around here? Is your home around here? Did your folks do this to you?" Her voice was soft but hard, if you know what I mean—like hair that looks good, but when you touch it, it's all hair spray and hard.

I shook my head. Things were clearing now, a little, and I could smell perfume on her, and it was the kind that doesn't cost too much.

"Ah, c'mon, Wanda." A man's voice, all brittle and tight, came from in back of her. "Leave it be, will you? You pick up every stinkin' stray cat and dog. . . ."

"Shut up, T-John." She sounded bored, as if maybe she was always telling him to shut up. Then she turned back to me. "You a runaway, kid?"

I didn't answer. I mean I didn't know who they were or anything. All I knew was that I'd done something good that was wrong, or something bad that was right, and these people might send me back to the farm. I didn't want to go back.

"Look, kid, we're carnies—carnival folks. Not cops. I want to help you, got it? Now, are you a runaway? Or do you live around here?"

It was all mixed up and I didn't understand anything, but I decided to trust her. "I'm a runaway."

I could see her head nod in the light from the truck. "I thought so. Now, who beat you up—was it the law?"

I shook my head again. "No—farmer. I was working for him."

"Damn." She said it so it wasn't like swearing but

just a statement. "You hear that, T-John? Some farmer did this to him. You hear that?"

"Yeah, I heard, Wanda. I heard." He sounded bored, too, as if he found beat-up kids on the road in the middle of the night all the time. "I heard."

"Listen, you two," the other man said, "maybe we ought to get going. Somebody will come along pretty soon, and what if it's a cop?"

"Shut up, Billy, and help me get him in the truck."

"Ah, Wanda, we can't take him with us," T-John said. "What if the law is after him?"

"T-John . . . " Her voice kind of hung there, like a sword.

"Okay, okay, but if you ever pull this again I'm going to grind you in the bullwheel."

Which didn't make any sense to me, but that was before I found that he ran the tiltawhirl and that the bullwheel was the big belt wheel underneath that powered the whole ride. I didn't know it, but T-John would never have put Wanda in the bullwheel or done anything else bad to her, because he loved her so much he would have eaten a mile of dirt just to lick her shoes.

But I didn't know that then and they sounded hard to each other, not mean but just hard.

"Come on, help me get the kid in the truck." She turned back to me. "Can you walk, kid?"

I nodded and stood up and fell over like a tree, my knees stiff. I can't explain it, but everything seemed to have gone out of me, like the stuffing running out of a doll. That's how it felt. And whatever it was that gave me strength to chop down Elsner and run across

the fields and get to the road just wasn't there anymore.

I bruised my nose when I hit the asphalt, and it
hurt, but only a little, and then I felt hands grab me
under the armpits. Another set grabbed my ankles,
and before I knew what was happening I was in the
truck where it was dark except for the light from the
dashboard instruments and where a radio was play-
ing country-and-western music and there was a faint
smell of beer.

Pretty soon there were people piled in all around
me so I was jammed kind of underneath the gear
shift, which stuck out of the floor and pushed over
against Wanda.

T-John was driving, and he put the truck in gear
and started down the road. I was squashed between
him and Wanda, and Billy sat next to her. As soon as
the truck got moving T-John reached down under the
seat and pulled out a beer can, which he gave to Billy.
Then he got another for himself. He didn't hand one
to Wanda.

I could see their faces better now, as my eyes got
used to the light and I wasn't blinded. T-John was an
older guy, maybe forty. He had a thin face and big
eyes and black hair and sideburns that came halfway
down his cheeks. When he took a sip of beer it was
professional looking, like he was sure of what he was
doing, and when he lit a cigarette he did it the same
way. Just snap and snap, and the lighter came up and
disappeared, and the cigarette glowed in the dark. He
drew deeply and blew smoke out sideways and tapped
his fingers on the wheel in time to the music, which

was Hank Snow singing about the big eight-wheeler moving down the track.

Billy, over by the window, looked exactly like T-John except that he was stone bald. There wasn't a hair on his head, not even eyebrows, and I found out later he was the geek in the carnival and shaved his head like that to look wild and mean. He sipped beer and smoked just like T-John, and you could see right away they were twins.

Wanda I couldn't see so well because she was turned to the other side, but I could feel her and smell her. She felt soft and hard at the same time, as if she were wearing a girdle and a hard bra, but didn't really need them.

For a long time nobody said anything, and finally T-John turned to me and said, "You hurt bad, kid?"

That surprised me, because I didn't think he cared whether I lived or died, after listening to him talk out on the road. I took a minute and shook my head. "No, I'm all right." Which was a flat lie, but I didn't want to look like a sissy.

"Bull." He laughed. It wasn't a mean laugh but soft, and I liked him right then, when he laughed. "But you're tough to say it—tough."

He fell quiet again, and nobody said anything for a long time. Then Billy offered me a sip of his beer. I shook my head and kind of leaned back against Wanda and relaxed.

"You want to talk about it, kid?" Wanda said into my ear. "Sometimes it helps to talk things out—clears the air."

"No—yes. I don't know." I didn't want to talk about

it, but I felt I had to, and pretty soon I was blabbing
the whole story about Elsner and the beets and the
snake and Maria and everything, and when I'd
finished I was crying again.

T-John flipped his cigarette out the window and
said, "Ahhh, people are such pukes, just turkeys and
toads," which was a code I didn't know yet, but which
meant they were dumb and worthless. "Reminds me
of the time I was down in Omaha near the stockyards
and these winos were cutting cows through the fence
for fun. . . . "

"Shut up, T-John."

And for once he did, and then there was only the
sound of the truck whining through the gears and me
sniffling, and finally I went to sleep against Wanda's
shoulder and I dreamed about Maria. I must have
cried some more because once when I came a little
awake Wanda had her arm around me and was
singing a country-and-western song.

I don't much like country-and-western music,
frankly, but I liked that, and it was good to hear as I
went back to sleep.

★11★

I slept like a stone, heavy and down, and when my eyes finally cracked the sleep away the sun was cooking through the windshield and the windows on the truck were open. For a minute I didn't know where I was, and I jerked around.

But Wanda held me down. "Easy, kid. It's all right." She scooched around so I could see her. "You're with friends."

"I didn't know where I was. . . ."

I felt all hot and sticky, and stiff as a rail. I could almost hear my bones crack when I moved, and my neck had a kink in it. Sleeping in a moving truck for seven or eight hours, sitting up, is like torture.

"Morning, kid." T-John was sitting next to Wanda and Billy was driving—they'd changed and I hadn't even known it. "You look like a blivet."

"Shut up, T-John."

"What's a blivet?" I looked out the window, and there were no beet fields, just prairie.

"A blivet is three pounds of slop in a two-pound bag." He laughed. "And that is how you look. Man, that turkey did a number on you, didn't he?"

I didn't say anything, but when he mentioned Elsner it brought it all back and I started to worry. I was a man on the run, and probably would have to hide out the rest of my life.

"Don't worry, kid." T-John read my mind. "I did a little checking last night at some truck stops, and you're clean."

"What do you mean?"

"I mean nobody is looking for you—no cops. At least not for murder. They might have a 'Wanted' out on you for running away from home, but that was a month ago and it's been forgotten."

"But—how could that be? I really hit him, and he turned belly up like the snake and everything. He must have been dead."

He shook his head. "Probably not. It takes a lot to kill a man like that. You'd be surprised."

"Even so. If I didn't kill him I came close to it. He'll tell the law. . . . "

"He can't." This came from Billy, who turned from the wheel and laughed. "You got lucky. The guy was running a wetback scam, working those people like that, breaking about fourteen federal laws. If he went to the cops they'd find out about the scam and hang him high."

"What does scam mean?"

T-John looked at me and shook his head. "Man, you have had one sheltered life, haven't you? A scam is what somebody does to pick up bucks, the way they operate."

"So you're smooth." Billy turned back to his driving. "But I wouldn't want to be any of those people back at the farm. He'll come down on them—hard. To make up for you."

I thought about that for a minute. "Then I'd better go back. I'll tell the law about him and get him stopped."

T-John looked at me as if I were crazy. "What in blazes *for*?"

"For Maria and the old man—all of them. If Elsner comes down on them . . . "

"Honey"—Wanda ruffled my hair—"that's what they call life. If you go back they'll only get it worse, have to go back to Mexico—not just the ones at that farm but all of them around there—and they don't want that. You'd just ruin it for them."

"So there's nothing I can do?" That didn't seem right because there should always be something you can do. "To help them?"

"Leave them alone." T-John reached under the seat and pulled out a couple of beers. He opened them and handed one to Billy and drank one himself. "Leave them alone—they're working their scam."

And it all made sense in an upside-down way. It wasn't right—it wasn't right that people could be used the way Elsner used them, like animals, but it made sense that I couldn't go back without messing it up for them.

We drove in silence for a while, and I moved up on the edge of the seat to give Wanda more room. Pretty soon T-John turned the radio back on, loud. I guess they'd had it off so I wouldn't wake up, and now it played the same country-and-western music.

I'd been watching the country, all pasture land and wide open, with some sheep but mostly cattle, and after a while I turned to T-John.

"Where are we?"

"Wyoming. We're going down to work a fair in Sundance; then we come back east and do South Dakota, then down into Nebraska." He pointed down the road with his chin. "Usually we don't go this far west, but Sundance has a big gig going this year, with a rodeo and horse show, and we figure to make some good money."

"Oh." I was thinking again, thinking that it might be fun to be with carnival people for a while, but I didn't know how to bring it up. I mean they'd been nice enough to pick me up on the road, and it didn't seem right to ask them if I could travel with them.

"Look, kid." He read my mind again. "I need a grunt for the ride. How'd you like to work with us for the summer?"

Wanda laughed. "I wondered how long it would take you to fish in."

"Pardon?" I turned to her.

"T-John—he was just like you when he was a kid. Took off because his feet were loose. I figured he'd fish in and ask you to work. I just didn't know how long it would take."

"Ahh, come on, Wanda, you know I need somebody to help me on the ride. Don't make more out of it than it is." He looked at me. "So what do you say?" I'll give you thirty-five bucks a week and all the food you can eat—carnie food, which isn't much, but it's better than beans and dry bread. Payday every Friday."

"I don't know anything about carnivals." I shrugged. "I mean I want to work for you, but I'd be pretty dumb. . . ."

"No sweat. I run the tiltawhirl—that's what's in back of this truck. All you do is help me set up and take tickets. You'll learn it in a day."

"Well, then, sure, I'll work for you. I'll be a grunt." I tried the word, which I wasn't going to ask about and look even dumber, but which I guessed meant a worker. "As long as you'll have me."

"And when you have some time off," Billy cut in, "you can shill for me on the geek show. I used to use Wanda, but now that she's running the saliva pit she doesn't have time."

Well, I wasn't going to ask about any of it—geeks or saliva pits—because I figured that was just their scam and I'd find out about it later.

Of course what it meant was that Billy bit the heads off of chickens and Wanda stripped down for the turkeys and toads.

But I didn't find that out until we got to Sundance and set up for the fair, the next day. Then I learned all about life and about how to make the seats in the tiltawhirl suck money and pull skirts up, which is all right but kind of dumb and gets boring after a while.

★ 12 ★

We got into Sundance, Wyoming, about two in the afternoon and I learned two things right away. When you work in a carnival, you *work*. Of course I didn't do much, still being busted up, but I helped where I could and when the pain let me, and we got the tiltawhirl up in about two hours. That didn't count putting in the seats that spin, which took a little more time. And then we put up the geek tent with Billy and the saliva-pit tent for Wanda.

The front of the geek tent was painted with a wild man with a huge mouth about to rip the head off a bird that looked like a chicken. Sort of. And over the top of the picture were the words:

SEE THE WILD MAN FROM THE JUNGLES OF NEW GUINEA! FOUND LIVING WITH THE APES! ONLY WEARS SKINS AND EATS BLOODY MEAT LIVE AND RAW!

By this time we had most of the stuff out of the truck, and I looked for the cage with the wild man, not yet knowing Billy was the geek. When I couldn't find anything I asked T-John about it.

"It's Billy. He covers himself with shoe polish and wears some goatskin and bites the head off a chicken now and then. They're wild for it. The turkeys."

"But won't they guess it's fake? I mean when they see Billy walking around loose?"

He nodded. "Yeah, but it doesn't matter. They still come because they don't believe he'll bite the chick-en."

When we got the banner up in front of Wanda's tent I had a little more trouble.

SEE IT ALL! It said, in pink and yellow letters. EXOTIC BEAUTY FROM THE EAST BARES ALL IN RITUALISTIC DANCE!

And below the headline was a painting of a woman with bare breasts wearing a grass skirt and waving her hands. I mean it really looked hokey and cheap.

"This is for Wanda?" I asked Billy, who was helping us and happened to be standing next to me.

"Yup. This is the saliva pit—what used to be called the hootchy-kootchy in the old carny days."

"But I thought—I mean, aren't Wanda and T-John like married or something?"

"Yup."

"Well. Of course I don't know anything, but doesn't T-John get mad when she takes her clothes off for other men like this?"

"You're right, kid. You don't know anything." His face got close and tight. "Maybe you'd better keep quiet about things until you learn something."

"Sorry." And I was, too.

"No sweat, but there's a lot you don't know about carnies and road folk. Here, sit down and let me tell

you what the score is so T-John doesn't have to cut
you."

I sat down on a corner of the box stand next to him.
His head was shining in the late afternoon sun, even
the shaved part covered with sweat, and he wiped it
with his sleeve before starting.

"See, it's like this: there are two different gigs
going all the time. Two different worlds. There's the
turkey world and the carny world, and what happens
in one doesn't matter a nickel's worth in the other.
Understand?"

I nodded, but I didn't really know where it was
going and told him so.

"Where it's going is that we're going to be here
three days, just three, and then we're going to move
on, and none of these people will see us again. Even if
they do see us again, next year, it'll be like they
didn't—they won't remember us. So what we show
them or what we do to them doesn't matter, see?"

"Yeah. Only all those turkeys seeing Wanda
naked, I don't understand how T-John can stand it."

"Because they don't matter. They're earth people,
and we're from outer space. Now if *I* took a look at
Wanda, or *you*—why, then, T-John would have to cut
us. Because we're part of his world."

He got up and left me sitting there, chewing on it,
and he was out of sight heading for the mess tent
before I thought to ask him about the cutting business. Did T-John carry a knife or was it some kind of
code word—I didn't know. I followed him and got a
chili dog, paying for it with the twenty I still had from
hitchhiking with the cowboy back before the beet
farm.

"Does T-John carry a knife?" I asked, my mouth full of hot dog.

"Is a pig's hind end pork?" He snorted. "We all carry knives. In our boots. That's why we all wear engineer boots."

I shivered. "Why knives? Isn't that a little mean?"

"A knife is the one weapon you hardly ever have to use—*because* it's so mean."

"But what if you do?"

"You talk *all* the time, don't you?"

"Sorry."

He looked over my head at the sky and then back down at the road. "In seven years with the carny I've only seen a knife used once, and that was by a dirt-mean man named Tucker when he cut up a kid. . . ."

His voice stopped. Just like that it stopped, and I thought maybe it was because he was mad at me or something. But when I looked up he was staring past me, over my shoulder, and when I turned, a tall man was standing there. He was thin and stood loose, but his face looked tight and I thought just then that if a snake ever turned into a man it would look like this. I almost moved away.

"Hello, Tucker," Billy said, only his voice was flat and hard. "We was just talking about you."

The thin man smiled—a slit opening and closing. "Nothing good, I hope."

"What are you doing here?" Billy stood up, and his body was tight like a spring. "I heard you were down in El Paso, licking saloon floors."

Tucker stiffened. "Keep talking, geek, and I'll give you your liver on a stick." His hand had moved to his pocket and so had Billy's, and for a moment I thought they were going to fight, but then Billy eased off and moved his hand back to his side.

"No trouble." Billy hissed the words. "Let's let it lie."

Tucker nodded and turned and walked off, as if he'd just dropped in for a how-de-do.

I found that I'd been holding my breath. I let it out. "Wow. What was all that about?"

Billy shook his head. "That was Tucker—and it was none of your business. Stay out of it. He comes from a long time ago and shouldn't be around here, and if T-John sees him they're going to tear up the turf. You tell T-John or Wanda he's here, and I'll bounce you like a ball. Got it?"

"But . . ."

"No buts. Tucker used to be with Wanda. He isn't anymore. You keep your mouth shut."

It wasn't enough, not for the way they'd looked at each other, but I knew I wasn't going to get any more, and besides, T-John and Wanda came walking up and she had a bag she handed me with a T-shirt and jeans and engineer boots inside.

"Go change," she said. "You look terrible."

I glanced down at myself on the way to the truck, and she was right. My clothes were half torn off. I changed in the cab, flattening down so nobody could see me. The jeans were a little loose, but the boots fit just right, and the T-shirt was perfect.

I jumped out and used the outside rear-view mirror to comb my hair. Then I went back to the two tents.

I wanted to know more about this Tucker business,

being just naturally curious but not nosy, but I knew it wouldn't do any good to push Billy. Besides, by this time the fairgrounds and shows were getting full and I wasn't carny enough yet to be cool about it. The whole thing excited me, so I pretty much forgot about Tucker, at least for the minute, and I walked up next to T-John where he was standing with Wanda and Billy next to the saliva pit. I was going to tell him that I thought I'd look around for a while, but they were all looking down the road, and when I looked down, I could see a cop coming toward us.

"He's after me," I said, and fear came up through my legs. "I just know it."

T-John laughed. "Naw—he's just checking the scams to see that they aren't too wild. Stay loose, kid. You'll see."

In a minute the cop was next to us, and he stopped. His eyes locked at T-John, and they studied each other for a minute. Then the cop pointed with his chin at the saliva-pit banner.

"Just show, right? No selling in back of the tent." He didn't say it mean, but just open—he wanted things to be understood.

"Just show." T-John nodded.

"You the geek?" The cop looked at Billy.

"Yeah."

"Rough way to make a living."

"Better than working."

They all laughed, and the cop nodded and walked on, and I breathed easier. He hadn't been after me, after all.

"All right, here's the action." T-John pulled us

around him. "They're opening the gates at five this evening, so we can get a little advance crowd tonight. The fair doesn't really start until tomorrow.

"Billy, I don't think there'll be enough time to work the geek scam tonight, so you wear a hat and work the saliva pit with Wanda. We might get one good crowd." He laughed. "At least some kids looking to see where they came from."

Billy and Wanda nodded and walked off. T-John turned to me, wrapped an arm around my shoulder and led me over to the tiltawhirl. He fired up the engine and threw the clutch lever so the seats started turning around and around, all empty, and he opened a beer and took a sip, and it hit me right then that I hadn't thought about the beet fields since before I saw the cop.

It was a nice feeling.

★ 13 ★

I learned something about people at exactly ten minutes after five, when we filled the tiltawhirl for the
first time, and by five-thirty I'd learned a lot more.

Something happens to people when they come to a
carnival. They change, and it seems their bad side
comes out—well, maybe not bad, but at least the side
they usually keep hidden.

Like the way girls acted. Those same girls probably
always were careful, but when they came to the
carnival and T-John started working the clutch lever
so the seats would spin harder and their skirts would
ride up, they would laugh and laugh and act embarrassed, even though they wanted it to happen.

Of course T-John didn't work the clutch for that
reason—that just happened. The reason he made the
seats spin harder was to make them suck money.

I watched him for a while, taking tickets and
working the little chain to hold the people back and

let them through, and it was plain to see that he was an artist at it.

He'd pick men with slacks on, not jeans, which a lot of cowboys wore. Then he'd wait until the seat was going over one of the high spots and he'd slap the clutch in and out and in again and spin the seat so hard you could almost see the brains come out their ears.

And that made the money come back out of their pockets, too, and fall down into the crack at the back of the seat. If T-John did it right he could drain their pockets, and empty them clean, so he didn't just get change but pocketknives and nail clippers and cigarette lighters.

The thing is, he did it all without looking—at least looking right at them. He stared out across the road and chewed gum and looked as if he couldn't care less about the people on the ride or the carnival or the whole world.

It was the carny stare, and when I started looking around I could see that everybody had it—at the other rides and the side shows. Even Wanda, who was across the road in front of her tent wearing a bathing suit and wiggling to the music from a loudspeaker under the stand, had the look—just staring off into nothing and not even seeming to notice the people gazing up at her body. It was a nice body, too, only a little heavy, and she had too much makeup on.

During a break when most of the crowd was working scams at the other end of the road I asked T-John about the look, and that's when he told me it was the carny stare.

"They want you to ignore them," he said. "It makes

them feel like dirt, and that's what they want to feel like when they come to the carnival."

"You're kidding."

He shook his head. "Nope—it's the truth. Just watch them. I tell you, kid, people are puke—those people, earth people."

"But that's sick."

He laughed. "Well, nobody said you had to be healthy to be an earth person."

That's how he explained the look, but I didn't go along with him, although I didn't say anything to him about it. I don't think the earth people wanted to feel like dirt, and I still don't—I don't think they're that sick, except for the ones like Elsner, of course.

I think they come to a carnival to have a good time and maybe let their skirts ride up because those are things they don't get to do when they're just living.

And I think the carny stare comes from the business of being two worlds. If the people working the carny looked right at the people and really saw them, it would bring the two worlds together, and then it wouldn't be right for them to see Wanda, and T-John would have to cut them.

But then what I thought and a dime, like T-John said, would get you a cup of coffee, if you were really lucky, so maybe it didn't matter. It was just that the stare was there, and even now when I go to a fair or carnival and see the carnies looking that way I think of the two worlds and how Tucker brought them together for T-John—the two worlds—so they had to fight and T-John had to kill him. . . .

But that wasn't for a few weeks, until the end of the summer, and I couldn't even guess it was going to

happen that first night. All I knew then was that
before the night was over I had the same stare, and
even if a skirt rode up I wouldn't look but would just
stand bored and let my eyes kind of glaze over.

And I didn't mean it to happen, either. It just did,
just came automatically, but before it came I had a
chance to watch down the road and see people acting
the way I used to act when I went to a fair.

There were the kids around the draglines, where
you paid a dime and worked little draglines to try and
pick up prizes in glass boxes. I used to do that when I
was a kid. Once I picked up a silver pony cigarette
lighter in a dragline, only it wasn't really silver, of
course, but chrome-plated cast iron, and the lighter
part didn't work. But I won it, and rather than take it
home I traded it in for five free plays.

That's the way the carnival scam really works.
They let you win a little, then take it back with more,
and when I was the kid working the dragline I
thought it was wrong, dead wrong. But now that I've
worked the other side I don't think it's wrong at all.

The carnival just lets the greed come out and work
against you, and in a way that's right, a good lesson.
That's what T-John said later, in Rapid City, South
Dakota.

"The best way to learn how to play poker is to lose,"
he said. "And the best way for them to learn about
greed is to let it hurt them. Shucks, kid, we're doing
them a favor taking their money—teaches them a
lesson."

"But they don't learn," I said. "They keep coming
back."

"Yeah." He smiled. "Too bad, isn't it?"

It was the same in all the side shows: the bottle swing, where you swing a ball out on a cord and try to knock a bottle over on the way back; the cat scam, where you try to knock over three stuffed cats with a ball, and the cats have weighted bottoms; the milk-bottle scam; the hammer-and-bell scam.

They were all the same. They worked on greed, so that the person getting taken had to be greedy in the first place or he wouldn't get nailed.

Of course I didn't see all this the first night but over a period of weeks, working all the towns. And it wasn't something I thought about all that much, if you want to know the truth of it—at least not that first night, watching all the cowboys and their girls and families and kids come into the carnival for a night of fun.

No, that first night, before I got the carny stare and learned to look but not look like I was looking, I just couldn't stop staring at all the people and thinking how normal they were. I think that got me more than anything—they all looked so *normal*—and I wanted to scream at them because of what was happening, because of Elsner and the beets and the Mexicans. With it all, how could they be so straight? But I didn't. I just watched T-John work the tiltawhirl to suck money, and pretty soon Wanda came back out on the stand in front of the saliva pit and after that I watched her because I'm just human, after all. Except of course I didn't do it so T-John would notice me.

She didn't dance so much as just move a little with her hips, and like I said before, she looked bored as all get out. And that's when I learned about sex, that first night, because when she first came out and moved with her bathing suit on, nobody stopped or looked much. Oh, now and then a cowboy would say something or stop, before his girl or wife would drag him on down the road. But even during the first act, Wanda only had a couple of guys follow her back into the tent to see her take her clothes off.

But for the second act Billy started to shill, which is to act like a customer who's really happy, and the way he carried on, whooping and making rude gestures and all, pretty soon there was a crowd in front of the tent.

And a lot of them followed Wanda in that second time, most of them young, like T-John had said, a couple of them younger than me, and that pretty much says it for sex. I mean it's all right, but it seemed people were sheep when it came down to cases, sheep who had to be told what to believe or be led down the path. "Led into the tent" might be a better way of saying it. It was disgusting—not Wanda, or sex, but the way they acted, the way they had to be shilled to do something they wanted to do anyway.

Out of the corner of my eye I caught T-John looking at me, and I forced a smile. "Turkeys," I said, pointing across the grass where they had followed Wanda into the tent and where Billy waited outside for the show to end so he could shill the next. "Just turkeys and toads."

He nodded. "You know it, kid. You know it."

And then he stopped the ride and I had to let the

next batch on for the next go around, some of them young girls who weren't ugly. And the rest of the night just went around in music and noise and the ride, with people going past every few minutes, and before long it all just mixed together until it was like I was in a loud and jangly dream.

★ 14 ★

"Hey, kid, come on, wake up."

I was really out. When we'd closed down the ride at ten o'clock I'd crawled into the front of the truck and sprawled across the seat with an old jacket over me like a blanket, and sleep hit me like an ax—just down and out—before I could think or anything.

Billy was pulling at my pants cuff and holding out a paper cup full of coffee. "Come on—they're slopping in the gedunk tent."

In back of him the sky was just getting gray. I squinted. "What time is it?"

"Up time. Come on, or we'll eat cold eggs." He backed off and I tried to sit up.

Every bone and muscle in my body screamed. I'd taken a set, like drying wood, and the beating had done enough so a night's sleep just let everything kind of settle in. I couldn't move my head, or my right arm, and when I winced Billy saw it.

He reached into the truck and pulled me out, slick as anything. "Move. Move around, jump up and down. Get loosened up or it will be a lot worse later."

I started to do what he'd told me, stopped when it hurt too much, then started again when he grabbed my hand and pulled me along.

"Hey, easy there," I said half in a whisper, hoping he wouldn't hear me, but I meant it. Moving hurt like blazes. It was almost worse than when Elsner had beaten me up. But Billy was right, and pretty soon, as we moved down the dusty grass of the road, the pain eased off some and I felt better. It was turning into stiffness, and even that had disappeared by the time we got to the gedunk tent, which was really only the food tent.

I still didn't know much about living carny—didn't know anything but what I was picking up from T-John and Wanda and Billy—so I had no idea what to expect at the gedunk tent.

The problem was that I was still kind of thinking like I had on the farm, at least in the back of my mind. I mean I knew there wasn't going to be boiled beans and dried bread, and I knew the plates wouldn't be nailed to the table, but down keep I was still back when I was hoeing beets. I was kind of like a dog that's been whipped down and isn't sure what to expect from a new master.

So I sort of hung back when we got to the tent, back by where the ropes came down to the metal bars they used for tent pegs, and sipped the coffee Billy had given me.

The inside of the tent was open, with the sides rolled up, but I couldn't see T-John or Wanda sitting anywhere, just Billy, who had a plateful of scrambled eggs he'd gotten from the cooks. He was sitting next to a young woman who was the daughter of the man who ran the Rocket of Death—I found later.

There were tables with benches out away from the cooking area, in rows, and I was just thinking of heading for one of the back rows and just sitting and watching things when Billy took his eye off the woman and looked to where I was standing.

He waved me over, and when I held back—I couldn't help it, I just got the stalls—he came over and got me.

"Look, kid, you can't act screwed up the rest of your life."

He dragged me over to the table and dropped me next to the young woman like a sack of flour, then went up to the cooks and came back with a metal tray covered with scrambled eggs and biscuits and two little cartons of milk and bacon.

It looked so good I almost forgot to be shy with the woman, which was just as well because she didn't want to see anything but Billy—bald as he was—and I might as well have been on the moon.

So I ate, only I couldn't get it all down and had to stop about halfway through. It was too rich, after all that straight beans and bread, and I could feel the sick coming on, so I stopped.

Then I sipped some coffee, which I don't normally like but which I figured it was time to learn about, and studied the people who were filling the tent. For a minute I didn't really see them, because I was miffed at the way Billy had treated me, dragging me around and plopping me on the bench like a kid. But then I knew he was just trying to help me, and the anger went down and I could watch the carny people. It was early enough in the day so they were natural and not like they would be when the turkeys and toads came onto the roads.

Mostly they were just ordinary people, who leaned to cowboy clothes and cowboy manners, and some of them were pretty and some of them were ugly. And they were all laughing and joking, and I found myself getting deep sad thinking about the Mexicans, who were silent when they ate and who had to work that hard. . . .

It wasn't right, not any of it. It wasn't right that the beet workers had to do that, and that they turned into what they turned into—not while there were normal things like this going on, where the people just joked and ate and threw away better food than I got to eat when I was hoeing.

I mean I almost got mad at the carny folks just for being what they were. It was that real, the way it came up in me. But I made it go down because it was just crazy, and that's when I noticed the difference in the way the carny people acted.

When there were turkeys and toads around they put on the carny stares, and that was one thing. But this was something else, something I couldn't quite pin down. It seemed that they were tight inside— tight and ready for something, even though there never was anything to be ready for that I could see.

The way you could tell was the way they held themselves when they walked, with their shoulders straight and level, and the way they always seemed to stand, as if they were expecting something bad to come. The women did the same as the men, and even a couple of kids had the look, which I probably wouldn't have noticed except that I still had a little stoop from hoeing beets and anybody who stood straight caught my attention.

But even with the tight look they were all happy. Billy and I had come earlier than almost everybody, so I got to see them coming into the tent, and they all joked and ragged each other in the private ways people who know each other have of doing. It was all loose and open, and in no time at all I started to feel the same way, open and nice.

I even started to enjoy the coffee, and by forcing myself I found I could sit straight, and if I kept my hands curved a little the calluses from the hoe handle didn't show. They were ugly, and I hadn't noticed them until just then when I'd reached for the coffee cup. The insides of my hands looked all lumpy and diseased, with thick skin and bulges of callus from the wear of the oak hoe handle. But like I said, if I held my hands in a curve, the calluses were hidden and I could almost sit straight.

I was just starting to enjoy not doing anything but watching people, relaxed and loose, when the girl sat down next to me.

"Hi."

She was all blond and clean and fresh and about fourteen or fifteen. She said it as if she'd known me forever, and I almost died inside. I mean I'm not normally shy, not really, but I wasn't ready just yet to climb right back into meeting people.

She startled me so I leaned over against Billy without thinking. He pushed me back hard enough so

I fell into the girl, and that just about tore it. Before I could think, I was up and out of the tent and trotting back to the end of the road with the tiltawhirl, so embarrassed I couldn't stand it.

And that was how my first day at the Wyoming Stock Fair in Sundance started, with me making a slab-sided fool out of myself worse than *any* turkey or toad.

And I didn't even get her name.

· 15 ·

Back at the ride I couldn't find anybody, namely T-John or Wanda, who were still asleep in the geek tent, so I busied myself cleaning the papers and stuff out of the ride. T-John had taken the money out the night before.

Everything was pretty grubby, and it took me half an hour to get it clean—thinking more about the girl than my work, the way you do when you've been dumb, coming up with a hundred or so things I should have said or done so as not to seem dumb. Even though I was.

When the ride was clean I went over to the saliva pit and went inside and checked it. The small stand where Wanda took off her clothes had been moved sideways a little so I straightened it, but the place wasn't dirty and I turned away and moved out fast. Somehow even being in the place empty seemed wrong to me—made me feel like maybe T-John wouldn't like it and would cut me.

Outside in the sun T-John came out of the geek tent scratching himself and rubbing his eyes, still half asleep.

"Morning, kid. You eat yet?"

I nodded. "Yeah. With Billy."

"Good. Why don't you take a minute and clean the ride up?"

"I already did."

"Oh. Eager, are you?" He smiled, looked up at the sun, and smacked his lips. "Going to be hot. Why don't you fill the canvas water bag at the front of the truck so we'll have it for the fainters."

I started off and turned. "Fainters? Who are they?"

"People who can't take the ride without passing out. When it's hot they seem to be the worst." He thought a moment, then added, "You'd better get the hose out, too. We might need it, if we can find a place to hook it up."

"What's the hose for?"

"Because it's going to burn off hot, like I said." He looked again up at the sun. "And when it gets hot we can have trouble—especially around the saliva pit. If we have the hose hooked up we can hose 'em down if we need to. So find it and hook it up to the nearest water tap, will you?"

I moved off, looking for the bag and the hose. The bag was hanging empty on the front of the truck, but the hose was in the tool box on the side. It took a minute to get it out, and in just that minute more people seemed to be moving down the road between the shows and rides.

Most of them were kids, ten and under, coming early to see if they could work their own scams—or that's how T-John put it later. All I thought at the time was that they all seemed to be wanting something to do to help get ready for the day, and I could see people at the other rides getting the kids to do their grunt work.

One of them came over to me—a skinny little guy with a grubby T-shirt and needing a haircut—and it kind of made me think of the way I used to be, back when I was a kid and the fair came to town.

Not too nice, is how it was, because I'd been poor, at least for fun money—still was—and I went to the fair early all the time when I was a kid to get work for tickets.

"Here, kid," I said to the skinny one, noticing a hole in the back of his T-shirt that he'd tried to cover with tape, "take this canvas water bag and get it filled. It's worth a free ride on the tiltawhirl when we get going."

He looked at me and flipped a smile and took the canvas bag, and I thought how cool I must look right then with the new Levi's and engineer boots and the tight T-shirt. I know that sounds like I was putting on something I didn't have, but that's the way I felt, and as I watched him walk away, I even felt kind of sorry for him because he was so far down the ladder. Which is just another way of saying you don't have to be smart to be a carny, as T-John would put it.

When he'd gone I turned back to the tiltawhirl. It was run by a gas engine, sort of a small-car engine, and I knew enough to check the water in the radiator, which was full, and the gas, which was almost all gone. I found a gas can on the back of the truck and filled the tank, and was just putting the can back when the kid returned with the water bag.

"Thanks," I said, taking it, not knowing then that you never thank grunts or workers like the kid. Billy told me later. "Another ride if you hook up the hose."

Again he flashed a smile and took off with the end of the hose, and I turned back to checking out the ride. Not that there was anything to do except just make-work, which I never did, and I was feeling sort of lost when Billy came back from the gedunk tent.

He had a cigarette in his mouth on one side and a toothpick on the other, and he talked right between them, standing with his back to the sun. It was up over the edge of the road by now and getting hotter all the time.

"Wanda out of the geek tent yet?" he asked. "You seen her?"

I shook my head. It was like the bit in the gedunk tent had never happened, like I hadn't gotten embarrassed and taken off, and for that I was grateful. "No. She's still asleep—or at least still in the tent."

He nodded. "That figures. She's probably putting makeup on—she can do that for a week. I'm going to prowl around the road for a while and see how the action smells. You find me as soon as Wanda gets out of the tent, because we have to get set up for the geek show." He stopped and studied me for a minute. "You all right?"

I nodded. "Sure. Why?" Dumb question.

"Just wondered. Want to hear a quick story? I mean a riddle."

"Sure." I was puzzled, but not about to let it show.

This whole business of acting carny was starting to get to me, and I tried to keep cool and smooth all the time so I wouldn't look like a turkey or a toad.

"Why is it that the biggest animal in the world, the flat-down and honkenest damn *giant* that ever moved on earth, the whale, only has a throat the size of a softball?"

I looked at him, thinking. Finally I shrugged and shook my head. "I don't know. Why?"

"Because that's the way it is, kid. That's the way it is." He smiled. "You get what I mean, kid?"

I looked at the ground. "Yeah. You mean how I acted at the tent. . . . "

"No. I mean the farm and the beet pickers."

"Beet hoers," I interrupted. "They don't pick, they hoe. To thin the beets out."

"Whatever. You see what I mean?"

I nodded. "Yeah. It's done, and there isn't anything I can do about it, right?"

"That's the ticket. That hand is dealt, and you lost. It's tough, but it happens. Throw it in and take a new deal—smooth out a little. You're walking freaked all the time."

He turned and walked off and left me standing there thinking about it. I was still a little weird in the back of my mind, kind of like there were corners that were still dark, and I knew it was the beet farm that was doing it—well, not the farm so much as Elsner and how he'd been. I wanted to forget it, and yet I didn't want to forget it, all at the same time, if you know what I mean. Maybe that's what they mean by growing up. I wanted to remember enough of Elsner and the beet farm so it would never happen to me again, but I wanted to forget enough so the pain would go away.

Maybe Billy was right and maybe everything happened because that's the way it was and maybe it was wrong to let things mess you up, but, by God, I wasn't ever going to get involved with another man the likes of Elsner. If remembering that made me weird it would just have to make me weird.

The kid came back right then and just hung around, and I didn't know what to do with him. It was sort of like having a pup, and I was just about to tell him to take off and come back later for his rides when Wanda came out and I sent the kid to find Billy.

Wanda looked neat, all made up and not a hair out of place and kind of hard but also soft. She gave me a hug, which was nice, and started off down the road toward the gedunk tent and I was left standing alone again. It hit me then that carny folks were about the most trusting folks in the world in an upside-down kind of way. I mean they were hard and worked all the scams to get money and never gave a sucker an even break, just like everybody thought. But all the same, T-John and Billy and Wanda would stop on the road in the middle of the night and pick up something like me and take me in, and then walk off and leave me alone to run the whole show and not know whether I'd steal and run away or not. Because when it came right down to the hair and the skin, they didn't know me from a fence-post hole on my uncle's farm, where I'd run off because there was no future there.

That made me some proud, and I looked at the ride and the pit and the geek tent, standing there in my new Levi's and T-shirt and slicked hair, like I owned them or something—proud and tall.

It was a good feeling, and didn't turn sour until I found that Billy had just gone out of sight and made a turn and watched me to see that I was honest, because carny folks don't really trust anybody but people they know, and they didn't know me.

But I didn't find that out until later when it didn't matter, because by then I'd turned into a carny person and knew what the scam was.

So I was standing there, all tall and loose feeling, when the blond girl came walking up. For a second I started to run, but then I thought of what Billy had said and stood my ground.

"Hi." She said it just like she had said it the time before, as if what happened in the gedunk tent never really happened, and she smiled so open and clean that I relaxed inside. It was like letting some of the air out of an overinflated balloon.

Then I answered her smile, and we talked for a while about junk that didn't matter, except that her name was Janet and she was my age and had been with the carnival since she was young.

I was just working around to asking her if she'd like to take a break from the carnival and maybe go to a movie in town when her dad came down the road and took her away because she had to shill and take tickets. But she waved, and I knew I'd get to see her again, which didn't make me feel bad, if you know what I mean.

★ 16 ★

Dust and heat and money.

That's what I think about when I remember what it was like that first full day at the fair in Wyoming.

By noon the road was getting packed with people—so many that you couldn't see them as people but only as colors and movement, and even that went away when the dust came up and stuck in the heat.

At first I helped T-John on the tiltawhirl, taking money and the tickets and holding the people back and letting them through, ignoring the screams when T-John worked the clutch for money.

But when the crowds got thick Billy gave me a sign, and I followed him around back of the geek tent, where he put makeup on and took his clothes off except for just a rag thing around his hips. Inside the tent there was a cage, and he got inside it with a couple of live chickens and a garter snake I didn't even know we had with us.

"Why the snake?" I asked.

"No reason. Just that snakes scare people, and that's what we want. When I get all settled you go get Wanda to run the show and then you shill by standing out in front on the road and looking eager. Got it?"

I nodded. "Yeah. But I'm not sure how I can look eager."

He smiled, which looked absolutely ridiculous—like a crazy minstrel actor trying to bare his teeth. "Think about that girl in the gedunk tent."

I blushed, tried to stop it, and felt it come through anyway. "That's not fair."

"Remember the whale. . . . "

"Even so."

"Go now, and get Wanda to start the show. Then get out front and shill." He made a face and jumped at me. "Before I bite off your head."

I jumped back and laughed. "That's wild, when you move like that."

"Wait until you see what happens with the turkeys and toads."

I went out front and found Wanda, who was in the truck relaxing. Later tonight she'd have to run the saliva pit, and between announcing for the geek show in the afternoon and stripping in the pit at night she needed all the breaks she could get.

"Don't tell me," she said, when I walked up beside the truck. "Let me guess. Billy is ready to run the geek show—right?"

"Yup. He's all made up."

"Ahh me, early morn to setting sun a woman's work is never done." But her voice was light, and she got out of the truck and worked through the crowd on the road to the little box under the banner while I stopped in front and let the people move around me. I know that's strange sounding, but that's the way it was with the crowds, as if they weren't real but just thick water or something. I looked up at Wanda, trying to seem eager even though I didn't think about the girl—well, only a little.

Wanda picked up the microphone and hit the switch. "DON'T GET TOO CLOSE!"

Some of the people slowed, and one or two stopped.

"HE RIPS THE HEADS OFF AND DRINKS THE WARM BLOOD!"

I mean it would have stopped a clock, let alone the turkeys and toads, and in no time flat there were people stopped and jammed up, with me in the middle.

"IS IT HUMAN OR IS IT ANIMAL?"

Now many of them were looking into the front of the tent, and they could see Billy back in the corner of the cage, kind of huddled down and looking dirty and greasy.

I mean it would have made you sick to see their faces, the way they didn't want to look but looked anyway—like they wanted to see what they didn't want to see.

Wanda went on and on with the pitch, telling them about the wild half-human and how it ate the heads off chickens and lived with snakes and all like that. And just when everybody was leaning forward to see into the front of the tent and the cage, Wanda pulled a rope and a canvas dropped over the opening.

"COSTS A QUARTER, ONE QUARTER, TO SEE THE WILD MAN FEED. DON'T COME IN IF YOU'RE SQUEAMISH!" Wanda raised her eyebrow and singled me out in the crowd and gave me a sign with her hand, kind of a forward motion. I reached into my pocket and dug out a quarter and stepped up to the stand.

"Me! Give me a ticket!" I mean I played it to the hilt. "I want to watch the wild man when he feeds!"

She smiled down and handed me a ticket and I went through, and you'd be amazed at what just one person buying a ticket like that could do. They were like sheep when the goat leads. Pretty soon they all walked up and paid a quarter—or a lot of them, at any rate—and they came crowding into the tent to stand next to me, staring into the cage at Billy.

Billy didn't look at any of them directly, except for one kind of pretty young woman who backed away when he smiled—maybe grimaced would be a better word—at her. Mostly he just sat, picking at himself and giving a first-rate imitation of a really bald monkey bored with everything. The chickens walked back and forth past him, as if they were fed up with everything, and the snake just lay coiled in a corner sleeping.

I found myself watching the people, studying them, and that's when I discovered the true secret of the carnival. They knew Billy wasn't a wild man from New Guinea, they knew it in their souls, but by paying the quarter they turned him into what they wanted him to be.

I know that sounds crazy, but it was true. I could tell looking at the crowd that they knew Billy was just as straight as any of them, but they *wanted* to see a wild man. That was why they'd come to the carnival. And because they'd paid a quarter, Billy really became wild for them in their minds.

"Back! Get back from the cage!" Wanda had finished selling tickets and had come into the tent. "He gets goosey when you get too close to his cage."

As if on cue, Billy half jumped up and made a growl in his throat, and I actually saw a woman in the rear faint and drop as if she'd been hit with an ax handle.

"All right, sir, give me that hat." Wanda took a hat from one of the audience. "Let's have a little more to see the wild man feed—just a little more nick in the knickers."

Her voice took on that sing-song sound of carnies when they throw the pitch, and I found out later that night that what she was doing was called the second touch, trying for more money before the act, and that they always did it. In the saliva pit when she took her clothes off sometimes she sent the hat around eight or nine times, once for each piece of clothing, and it always came back with money in it.

This time it went around just once, and she expertly took the money out of the hat and made it disappear. Then she took a stick from the corner and poked it through the bars and nudged Billy in the ribs.

He growled some and took a couple of swipes at the stick and settled back in the corner.

"Come on, *eat,* you miserable beast!" She took a few more pokes, and Billy hung back. She got up beside the cage, and he jumped at her and grabbed at her clothes, growling like a dog. It even scared *me,* and I knew it was fake. A couple of the men in the audience moved forward to help Wanda get away, and another woman fainted. But it was only fake; she came to right away.

Billy moved back in the corner of the cage and sat again, but this time he looked at Wanda and the stick and looked scared. Then before anybody knew what was happening, he grabbed a chicken and held it up in front of his mouth.

It squawked and kicked and tried to get away, and he opened his lips and bared his teeth, and if you'd asked me right then, at that instant, I would have told you that there was no way in the world Billy would bite the head off that chicken. Not even for money, not even for the scam.

But he did.

His teeth flashed, and the head was gone, and he spit it out in a corner of the cage and let the blood spurt out of the neck of the chicken onto the clothes of people in the audience who had moved too close when he grabbed the chicken in the first place.

The blood went out like a red rain, and the chicken's wings splattered it around. Some of the crowd screamed, and some of the others upchucked. I was just barely holding control of my own stomach and mind when I looked at the corner of the cage and saw the chicken's head down there with the eyes opening and closing and the mouth opening and closing even though it was cut off and detached from the body where Billy had spit it.

It was more than I could take. I thought of Elsner when I hit him with the hoe, and of the snake, and that chicken just kept opening and closing his mouth and eyes, and the heat in the tent and the screams of the women in the crowd came barreling into my thinking and I went down like a yoyo that was never going to come back up.

★ **17** ★

When I came to, I was in the back of the tent. All the people were gone, and Billy was out of the cage and smoking a cigarette between gigs.

Wanda was kneeling over me with a worried look on her face and she had my head in her lap.

"Are you all right?"

I nodded. "Sure. It must have been the heat. I just passed out."

"Good. I mean that's not good, passing out. It's good that you're not hurt or anything. You take the rest of the day off."

"Aw, Wanda . . . "

"Listen to her, kid," Billy cut in from across the tent. "She knows what she's talking about."

I shut up and got to my feet. I was a little woozy, but after a couple of seconds I felt fine. "See, everything's okay."

"Just the same, cool it for a day."

"I'll just help T-John on the tiltawhirl." Outside I
could hear the crowd screaming and the sound of the
engine on the ride going faster and slower as T-John
worked the clutch for money. "He's pulling double
work right now, running the ride and taking tickets.
Don't worry, I'll be all right."

I got out of the tent before either of them could
object and moved across the stream of people in the
road.

Outside it was hot, so hot I could hardly breathe,
and I pulled a few deep breaths before walking up to
T-John.

He was busy as a cat on a cement floor, but he still
noticed me.

"What happened? You look like you died and came
back." He was drenched with sweat, and a cigarette
hanging out of his mouth had gotten so soggy it was
starting to fall apart.

"Nothing. Just got a little sick."

"Can you work?"

I nodded. "Sure."

"Take tickets and work the chain."

I moved into position on the chain and was no more
than settled when the kid I'd sent to fill the water bag
came up asking for his free rides.

I nodded, hard and tight, without really looking at
him, the way I'd seen carny people do, and let him
through first when the ride stopped and the next load
wanted on. When he got done I asked him if he
wanted to make a buck, and he said sure, so I sent him
over to Wanda to shill for the geek show and I was on
top of it.

I mean, by that time, in that short a space, that first full day in Wyoming, I was carny.

It's kind of hard to explain, how it could happen so fast, but between passing out when Billy bit the head off the chicken and moving across the road to help T-John I'd changed and become carny.

Like when the kid came up and demanded his free rides and I let him on, I *knew* that I would ask him to shill and offer him a buck, and it wasn't something I had to think about but something that just came out.

I was carny.

And it was all right, felt really good, to be so sure of myself. I felt all easy and free and stood working the chain and taking money and giving out tickets and pouring sweat, just like T-John, and when it got dark Wanda sent the kid down for some chili dogs, and I ate one while I worked.

After that I drank a Coke with crushed ice, and the people just kept coming like a bunch of fish. And once, when I happened to look across the screaming kids and tired parents—I don't know when but it must have been nine or ten that night—T-John was looking right back at me, and he smiled, his face dripping, and it was a secret smile just between two carnies, just between two men. I answered it with a smile and a wave, and that was all right.

Because if the truth were known I wasn't all that sure that T-John wanted me around even though he'd hired me. He was so tough and he had griped so much when Wanda made him take me off the highway that up till that night I think I still thought he might just have hired me to keep Wanda happy.

But the smile changed that. It was just between us, like I said, between two men working a tiltawhirl ride in the middle of the summer on a hot night surrounded by turkeys and toads. . . .

It was all right. It made me belong.

And even later, when Wanda started up the saliva pit and the crowd started to get out of hand and we had to use the hose and the cops came to help out— even through all that I felt that I belonged. And I think that was when I decided that all I wanted for the rest of my whole life was be a carny, because I fit in so well and it had a future that I wouldn't have back on my uncle's farm. I belonged.

I mean, it didn't hit me that fast, but sort of just came over me so that it was something I felt more than knew. Like when Wanda did the first pit show and took it all off and it was hot and loud and a crazy cowboy started screaming and wanted to tear the place apart and we fired up the hose and settled things down—I was the one who got the hose out. Just like I'd been doing it all my life. And I knew just how to spray it around and hit the heads so the people would cool off.

"Good work, kid," T-John said when I'd finished and most of the people had moved off. "Nobody hurt or even mad. Good work."

Which naturally made me feel ten feet tall.

And still later, when we had a woman catch too much heat and excitement on the tiltawhirl and fall over, I knew how to dampen a rag and wipe her on the forehead and bring her back out of the faint and get her off the ride without taking up too much time and it costing us too much money.

And again T-John flipped me a smile, a secret grin. "Looking good, kid, looking good."

And I was, too—looking darn good. I had it by the tail, holding tight, riding it all the way to the top.

I was carny, and I decided right then to stay carny for the rest of my life, and it didn't matter that people thought carny folks weren't respectable or nice. That didn't matter at all. I knew better. I knew they were the only people on the face of the earth who were real. I knew that being carny was the only way to live, the only way to have a future.

It was a great feeling. It was knowing that I wouldn't run when a girl sat down next to me and said "Hi," knowing that I wouldn't puke or pass out when Billy did the next geek show and bit the head off a chicken, knowing that I wouldn't be shocked thinking about Wanda taking off her clothes for the turkeys and toads; it was knowing that I knew me.

Lord. That was all right. I worked that night as if I owned the tiltawhirl, even changing places with T-John and working the clutch for money and looking bored.

Looking carny.

It could have gone on forever, that first night when I found out all about myself. It could have just gone on and on, and I wouldn't have minded.

To show you how good it looked and felt, I was so cold blindsided that I didn't even notice the change in the air when a tall, thin man with a cowboy hat

walked past the ride and moved on down the road. I
mean I saw T-John look at him long and tight, but
then the tall man was out of sight and gone, and the
people kept coming and the ride and the noise kept
going, so nothing seemed out of place in the incident.

As a matter of fact, if you'd *told* me that the man
who went by was Tucker, who he was, and had sat me
down and forced me to listen about how Tucker and
T-John had bad blood from years before, and how
Tucker was poison-mean, like Billy had said—if
you'd *made* me listen to all that, which was all
true—I wouldn't have paid much attention.

Not that night. Not right then. I was carny. And it
was looking *good*.

⋆ 18 ⋆

"I read somewhere that South Dakota is going into a drought." T-John lit a cigarette and took a sip of cold beer from the can he held between his legs while he drove. "I believe it."

Nobody argued with him. We'd just finished a county fair outside of Rapid City, the fourth in a row since we left Sundance, and were on our way to another small show in the center of the state. I didn't know the name of the town.

Not that it mattered. I'd been with T-John and Wanda and Billy through five shows, and they'd all been in South Dakota but one, and after the second one I couldn't tell the difference because there wasn't any difference to tell—they were just shows. Traveling between towns was just a long hot run across flatness through miles of short burned grass and soft sticky asphalt to set up the rides and tents in dust and heat and noise.

I was sipping a pop, cold, because I didn't like beer—couldn't stand the taste of it. The truck wasn't too crowded, because Billy was riding with the people from the rocket so he could be with his new girl. I might have been riding with Janet, because we were getting closer, but we weren't so close that I could sit with her folks yet. I thought about her a lot when I couldn't see her, which is pretty dumb, but that's the way I am.

"I was a kid down in Oklahoma during the dust bowl," T-John said, looking at me, and I could see Wanda get a bored look on her face because she'd heard it all before. "Me and Billy—we were just tadpole kids then and didn't know what it was all about except that we were poor and it was hot and dusty so bad you couldn't make spit."

He took a long drink of beer, remembering, and I wondered how he could drink so much of it and never get drunk. He went through can after can, popping the tops and chugalugging the beer down, then flipping the empties out the window and letting them roll after us on the highway until they stopped.

Wanda cleaned between her teeth with a long fingernail, only it didn't look bad, kind of natural.

I looked again at T-John. "It was bad?" I asked, to nudge him.

"Yeah." He nodded. "I've never seen anything like it. Pa, he died pulling his guts out on a toothdrag because the horses died of the heaves. He thought if he pulled the drag across his fields sideways it would stop them blowing away." He stopped and for a moment looked down the highway, thinking, his eyes glazed. "Think of that—a man dying pulling his guts out in a harness, doing work an animal should do. God."

I thought of it, but frankly it didn't get me all that much. I mean it was sad, but I'd hoed beets, and after that nothing is bad.

"Ma didn't die, not then," he started again. "But we had to send her away to the state hospital."

"What happened?" I couldn't help asking.

"Something in her mind just broke." He shrugged. "I was too young for it to stick—just sort of remember when it happened. One morning she opened the icebox after it had been blowing hard for three or four days, blowing dust and sand, and she got the door open and the icebox was full of sand—*inside*. And the doors had been closed. She couldn't stand it, couldn't take it, and she just sat down on the floor and cried and cried. . . . "

He let it trail off like that and went inside himself. For a while I thought he was going to go silent, but after a bit he gave a little laugh that wasn't from humor. "There wasn't nothing good then—nothing good in those days. Even the people were mean—sad or mean. Nobody smiled and nobody was good."

Wanda flashed him a look but didn't say anything. I waited, listening. Hot air came through the cab, and he moved to ease the sweat of his back against the seat. Then he took another snort of beer.

"Tucker." He said the name hard and cold, like glass breaking. "He came from the dust back then. Tucker came from there, and he's all mean and needs to be ended."

This time Wanda's eyes were worried, but still she didn't say anything.

"He came through the road the other night," T-John said to the windshield, and I could feel Wanda stiffen. "Tucker came through, and when I saw him I started looking down old tunnels. But then he moved on and I let it hang. . . . But I should have cut him."

Tucker again. I remembered the cowboy who had come by the ride. I started to ask about him, but T-John had gone back to driving. I stared down the same road, knowing that he was remembering something he didn't want to remember, the way I sometimes did when I thought about Elsner and the beet farm.

"Kept picking at it, didn't you?" Wanda asked, across me. She might have been nagging, except that her voice was soft and wise sounding, and I knew she wanted to help him through it, through thinking about his father dying pulling his guts out and his mother going crazy with dust in an icebox and Tucker and all of it.

"Yeah."

"T-John, when you gonna learn to leave the past alone?"

"Gimme another beer." He threw a can out the window, but I knew it wasn't all empty yet and that he was just doing it to have something to do. "And turn the radio on."

She opened a can and handed it to him, then turned the radio on and played around with the dial until she got some western music. We all leaned back and listened, humming and tapping time with our feet and hands, and after a while the bad picture of T-John's parents went away, at least for me, and it kind of felt like we were a family or something.

I mean I know that sounds dumb, especially for someone who's gone off to seek his future and fortune, whichever comes first. But if the truth were to come out, when you aren't completely grown up and haven't got all your meat on your bones just yet—even when you're seeking your fortune—being all alone can be kind of a problem.

Not that I couldn't make it alone, understand. But it felt just a bit better sitting between T-John and Wanda, knowing they were there to kind of watch over me—like having friendly bookends or something.

That just made it easier all the way around, so that I could let my mind get loose and travel around in all those nice places you don't always get to go in when you're alone and seeking your fortune and future, and I let myself imagine we were a family or something. Pretty dumb, I'll admit, and normally I wouldn't have let myself go on that way, but I'd noticed that as we went from show to show, T-John seemed to be taking a liking to me. I mean I knew he didn't have any family but Billy and Wanda, and no kids—that he knew about, as he put it—so it wasn't all that far off to think of being with him like a family.

I pretty much ran the whole ride by myself, after picking up a grunt from the kids who hung around, and I noticed that it gave T-John more time to help Billy and Wanda in the geek and saliva shows—made everything run smoother.

"I don't know much," T-John said, suddenly, tapping time to music on the wheel, the wind whipping through the cab, "but I don't want it to wind up being a sad story for me the way it was for my folks. I mean when it's done I don't want some bastard sitting in a truck going across South Dakota to feel bad about how I lived. . . . "

I turned to look at him and was surprised to see the corners of his eyes soft and wet—either from the wind or from crying—and it struck me funny that he could keep tapping time on the wheel if he was feeling sad about his folks.

But he must have, because Wanda saw it, too. She reached across me and put a hand on his arm and gave him a tender look that somehow seemed to take me in as well, and even though it was a kind of sad moment I felt warm inside.

Then it was over, or gone for the time anyway, because down the road we could see the tall white grain elevators of the next town, where we were going to set up for a county show and take the turkeys and toads.

Or at least that's what I thought. We were barreling out of the west down on this town, and I honestly didn't think it was any different than the others.

We had our world and it was private and getting nicer all the time, at least as far as I could see. We were going into another town where the turkeys and toads had their own world, and we could keep ours. And I had a future and a fortune started because T-John was paying me steady. . . .

I mean it was all working out. Even the sad parts were warm, like when Wanda kind of took me in when she reached out to help T-John.

I didn't want for anything else—that's how good it felt right then. And to show you how stupid a person can be, I almost felt sorry for the town up ahead. It wasn't just another show coming down on them, but a carny family all close together and tight and ready.

I almost felt sorry for them.

Of course that was before I found out how Tucker would bring the two worlds together for T-John. He would bring them together so it was like a collision of fire that wouldn't leave anything but ashes and turn my future and fortune into a bad taste in my mouth.

That was before I knew Tucker would pick that town to come out of T-John's life back when he was young and wiry, to come out of the past like a ghost and pull the two worlds together. They would have to dance with steel, the two men, and ruin everything so that I had nothing to do but what was good for me.

And doing what is good for you is always the worst thing. Even if it works out all right in the end, it is the worst thing when it first happens—just the way things that seem good for you can turn out bad, bad as dirt.

But for now we came toward the town across the prairie that went on forever and, like I said, I almost felt sorry for them as we wheeled down the hot asphalt like a hot arrow. Almost felt sad about taking all the turkeys and toads.

★ 19 ★

By now we had a routine worked out so we could get
set up in record time, and at first it seemed like any
other show.

T-John warped the truck into the right place and
jerked the tailgate while I got out and scammed a
couple of grunts from the kids. Then he started setting up the ride while I worked with Billy and
Wanda, getting the geek tent and the saliva pit up.
That took just a few minutes, and then I moved back
to help T-John finish up the tiltawhirl, and just like
that—in nothing flat—we were all set up.

Almost before we'd really even arrived, T-John and
Billy were having a beer, watching the evening sun,
and Wanda was sipping a drink with ice she'd gotten
somewhere. I was drinking a Coke.

Everything was finished. The show didn't start
until eleven the next morning, and I was just thinking of ambling into the small town—I still can't

remember its name—when Janet came walking down the road.

"Heads up, Grunt," T-John said. He often called me Grunt. "Love coming at you."

Well, naturally I blushed, but I was over being dumb and I walked out to meet her. She was pretty, like I said before, and the rest of that night would seem pretty boring unless you were personally involved, if you get what I mean. Actually it wasn't boring at all, and everybody in the world seems to like to hear about the sort of evening Janet and I had. But to describe it is boring and what T-John would call low, because real men never talk about those things. They don't have to.

Without going into details, I'll just say I came back to the ride and tent about midnight. I was tired and I guess kind of in love, if you can be kind of in love, and there were things in my mind I didn't understand. But that was all right.

T-John was standing by the truck when I got back. "Evening." He said it flat and straight. "Have a nice time?"

I nodded. "Great. I mean . . . "

"I know what you mean. You don't have to explain." He looked at me across the pale light that came from the other rides that were being set up on the road. "Don't let it throw you. What happened tonight out there with Janet"—he aimed a chin at the rest of the world—"it's just part of living. Don't let it make you go crazy."

I nodded, but I didn't really understand what he meant—still don't. Of course that might be because I was in love, at least right then.

"Go to bed now," he said, after a moment. "We gotta hump tomorrow and I'll want you to run the ride alone."

I moved off and curled up in the blanket roll Wanda had gotten for me. I would have spent more time trying to think about what T-John had said, but all I could think of was what it had been like with Janet, and I fell asleep smiling and thinking that finding your future and fortune and fame was pure quill fun if you found somebody like Janet to go with it.

Morning was normal, too. I hit the gedunk tent before anybody else came, but even though I stayed for extra coffee and a fourth doughnut, Janet didn't come, so I was a little disappointed when I went back to the rides.

Kids were everywhere, and I nailed a couple for help for the day. After that I had the kids get the water and hook up the hose, just in case, and I checked the ride to make sure it was all right.

It was about eleven in the morning, just coming up on noon, when the police came to check things out. I held my breath, still being a runaway and all, but they just talked to T-John and made sure the saliva pit was for show only and I breathed easier. If they checked me out I'd have to go home, because I was on the runaway list, but unless they made the effort I was all right.

At noon I started the ride, wheeling it around empty a few times, then giving some of my grunts rides to pay for the work they were doing for me—using them as shills was what I was doing. That brought a few people down, and I got them on the ride and didn't work the clutch for money but left it nice and gave them a long ride. That brought still more customers, the way it always does, and by one o'clock in the afternoon I was so busy I didn't have time to blink.

About one thirty, when it was getting really hot and I was thirsty enough to hurt, Janet came by with a smile and a large Coke with crushed ice and my world filled right out.

For the rest of that afternoon it couldn't get too hot and the turkeys couldn't get too dumb and nothing could go wrong, I knew it. And when evening rolled around and Wanda got the saliva pit going and Billy and T-John worked a crowd up around the geek tent, I could see we were really going to clean up. We had the best crowd I'd ever seen, even though the town was kind of small. They were all rich wheat farmers who'd just sold their crops, and they were spending money like it was water. I wasn't sure, but I thought I might have upwards of fifty dollars in the seats—just by working the clutch—and I knew I had over two hundred in the cash box under the engine controls by seven o'clock. At eight, when it got dark, I topped three hundred, and it was coming on being a rich night because the saliva pit and geek tent were packed all night.

I mean they'd come to *spend,* those farmers, and we were just helping them out. I've never seen anything like it. Once I saw a woman who got sick during the first geek show when Billy bit the head off the chicken go right back for the second show and get sick all over again. She paid for it twice, too.

And there were men who just stayed in the saliva

pit for show after show, paying over and over. It was just crazy, because if you've seen a naked lady once, why pay to see the same one again? But they did, and that's where I first noticed the cowboy.

I was fairly numb with working and it was dark, so it must have been about eight-thirty that night when I looked from the tiltawhirl across to the saliva pit where Wanda was dancing. I didn't look up but just over, didn't look at Wanda, and there was this guy in a tall cowboy hat, tall and with a wide, curved-down brim.

Again, I wouldn't have noticed him at all, except that he had a big eagle feather in his hat, and I thought how sad it was that an eagle had to die for the feather to be in his hat. Then I saw that he wasn't looking at Wanda but at T-John.

And T-John was looking back at him.

You could tell two things right away, so plain it was like daylight. Even with the crowds, and even in the dark, T-John and the cowboy *knew* each other, and the cowboy was Tucker, and they didn't like each other.

At *all*.

I mean I've seen men mad and mean mad at each other and know how their shoulders stiffen up when they hate deep, but this was worse than that—this was deeper hate than I've ever seen.

T-John was up on the stand in front of the geek show, waiting for Wanda to drum up a crowd before he moved in to take tickets and run the saliva pit for her, and I thought for a second he was going to come off the stand and land on the cowboy with the eagle feather in his hat.

But Billy had been down in front and had seen the look and said something from below that made T-John stop and hold back.

Right then the cowboy made a big thing out of looking away from T-John, and for a minute I thought it would be all right. I thought maybe whatever it was between the two men that could cut through noise and crowd that way had died before it could get going.

Then the cowboy looked up at Wanda, who had that bored look dancing and hadn't seen anything pass between the men, and he smiled wide and dirty. There was no mistaking the look. He meant to pay and go in and see Wanda without her clothes.

He meant to do that, and he knew T-John could no more take that off a man than he could die—he'd *rather* die—because that brought the two worlds together, made it all wrong. And so you could say T-John had to do what he did—to save his way of life.

He screamed a swear word that cut through the air like barbed wire and came off the stand through the crowd, which was already moving away. And when he got close to the cowboy he reached down into his boot. There was a flash and he had his knife out, the knife he never really meant to use, the knife that was mainly to keep crowds and turkeys and toads from getting out of hand. That knife.

He pulled it and flashed the blade and stopped, looking at the cowboy.

"Fill your hand, Tucker," he said, and that's when I knew everything was going wrong. "Fill your hand or I'll gut you like a fish where you stand."

And the cowboy filled his hand.

⋆ 20 ⋆

Wanda screamed, which didn't seem right, and then she ran back into the tent. The crowd moved apart but didn't run. They just made a circle around the two men, who stood half crouched with their knives, silver death in the light from the road—and they waited.

I had a picture in my mind right then, a kind of flash, and the picture was like a movie of what was happening and what would happen—like, if they fought with knives and it got out of hand, the police would come. They would investigate all of us, and they would find out I was a runaway and it would all have been for nothing, all for nothing. I would have to go back to my uncle's farm and settle down and farm the land he wanted to give me.

"No!" I screamed across the crowd. I left the til-tawhirl and started over to get between them, bust-ing through the turkeys and toads like a machine, until a set of hands stopped me.

"Hold it, kid." It was Billy, and he held me cold. "Stay out of it."

"But they're going to fight—going to get in trouble."

Billy nodded, looking at T-John and Tucker. "Probably. Tucker did some dirt to T-John. They have to fight—that's what Tucker is doing here. He's come to find out T-John and settle it. Leave them to it, kid."

"But we have to stop them. . . . "

"No." Billy moved as other people in the crowd nudged him to get a better view of the fighters. He swore and pushed the turkeys away. "Tucker was going to go in and watch Wanda—that's too much. Before that I tried to stop T-John, and he was cool, but after that he has to cut Tucker or lose everything. Lose what he *is*. Now shut up and watch. You might learn something about fighting."

I tried to bust loose anyway, break into the closed circle and stop the fight, but Billy grabbed me and held me. All I could do was watch, and that was terrible because it wasn't anything like I thought but much worse.

They didn't square off or even much look as if they were fighting. Instead the knives just kind of licked out like the tongues in snakes, so fast they just flicked.

And each time they flicked there was blood. I've never seen anything like it. T-John just sort of twitched with his arm and a line of red appeared on Tucker's cheek, and the line turned to a smear and the smear turned to a flow of blood down his neck while I watched.

Then Tucker sort of shrugged his shoulder and a cut went down T-John's arm below the T-shirt sleeve, and pretty soon there was blood all over the place. I've never *seen* so much blood.

The crowd was quiet, and when I happened to look at some of them because they got in front of me, it was enough to make your guts curl. Their eyes glistened the way they did when Billy got ready to bite the head off the chicken; they were all shiny and wet, and you could tell they thought they shouldn't watch, but they did watch anyway, couldn't help it.

And it was silent—just deep silent with the only sound coming from T-John and Tucker as they grunted and breathed and lunged.

I mean I don't know what I expected, but I know it wasn't a silent fight like this, all eerie and quiet and spooky so that even the road seemed to get quiet. All the other rides came to a stop and finally the til-tawhirl itself stopped when one of the grunt kids pulled the clutch handle. Even the noise of the rest of the carny folks working their scams and running their pitches stopped when they heard there was a fight going on down by the saliva pit, and it became as quiet as if there were no show at all.

I think I wanted T-John to swear and act mad, or have Tucker be mean, but nothing like that happened. They just circled each other and the knives kept darting out, licking little lines of blood. Pretty soon the ground was wet with it, and some of the watchers got some on their clothes. T-John and Tucker were just red from head to foot, all red.

That's when I saw the cop. He came up on the other side of the circle and stood there for a moment, watching the fight. Then he looked across at Billy because he knew Billy was T-John's brother, and Billy gave the cop some kind of look I didn't understand. The cop shrugged as if to say he'd wait until the fight finished before he checked things out. Then I saw him look at me, and study me, and I knew he was remembering that I was with T-John, and I could just see the wheels turn in his head.

I was cooked. Sure as anything, he'd run a check on me and I'd have to go home and run the farm for my uncle. I started to run, started to break out of the circle and run from the cop, but then I looked back at the fighters, looked at the blood and saw how Tucker was getting weaker, how his eyes were starting to slide back in his head. I knew he was dead, and something in me kind of slipped.

I mean I thought that if this was part of my fame and fortune maybe I didn't want any of it. Even Janet and what had happened with her the night before and the fact that I was getting rich—maybe all that wasn't enough to overcome what was happening out in the circle of turkeys and toads, because the blood now was all over the ground and over both of them. Even Janet and the money couldn't make up for the way Tucker was sliding down and down as T-John's knife carved him up, and when he finally hit the ground and goobered and was dead I knew I wasn't carny.

Not really.

I turned and looked up at the stand on the saliva pit where Wanda had come back out to see the end of the fight, because she was worried about T-John. She caught my glance. She must have known that it was over and that I had to leave, because she reached out.

Nice, that hand, because it came out just a little and across the crowd of turkeys and toads. It wanted to help me stop the hurt but it didn't—help, I mean—and I looked back to where T-John stood over Tucker, who was down and dead, and there was nothing in the world for T-John but the body right then—the body and his own wounds.

Then Billy left my side and walked into the circle and caught T-John just as he started to fall. And the cop went in to arrest T-John, and I walked in to tell the cop that I was a runaway, because it was over, all over, over and done like the beets and the snake and Elsner, and the blood in the dust of the carnival road, and the body of Tucker all still and curled in a red and gory ball. And it's kind of funny, but I felt good that it was over.

Sort of, anyway.

Because in the end it's like T-John said once: some people like thunder and some like the rain. And not everybody likes the thunder and not everybody likes the rain. Going off to seek my fame and fortune was maybe like tasting the thunder, even though I'm a person who likes rain best.

Maybe.

At least that's what I tell myself now when I wake up and the damp is on my face and it takes me a minute to remember that I'm home and running a farm and liking rain and not tasting thunder, and that T-John and Wanda and Billy are all in back of it now, in back with the part of my life where I went off to seek my fame and fortune and find out about love and sex and death and what it's like not just to be a man but to kill a man.

They're in back of me now, and like my uncle always says, done is done. Maybe he's right, but I doubt it, because to say done is done is like saying you're supposed to forget all about what happened. It's one of those things that're awfully easy to say and very hard to do, and it's especially hard when what you're trying to forget is Tiltawhirl John and Wanda and Billy the geek and the beet farm and Janet. . . .

Maybe done *is* done.

But I doubt it.